CHASING WINDMILLS

CHASING WINDMILLS

A Novel

MICHAEL T. HEMENWAY

Lightfoot
Press

Copyright © 2025 by Michael T. Hemenway.
Front and back cover art by Michael T. Hemenway.

Lightfoot Press
Charlottesville, VA

Printed in the United States of America

ISBN: 979-8-9990613-0-0

To my grandsons

CHAPTER 1

BOOKS

The day the class started *The Old Man and the Sea*, it was raining, the kind of steady Virginia fall rain that made the classroom windows blur like impressionist paintings. Most of the class was half-asleep, lulled by the weather and the prospect of another assigned reading. Sam was sketching motorcycle engines in his notebook, something he'd started doing after spending weekends in his grandfather's garage.

Dr. Fitz's classroom was the only one in Summit High without motivational posters. Instead, the walls held weathered maps from places Sam had never heard of and black-and-white photos of writers who looked like they'd rather be anywhere else than in front of a camera. Fitz's desk was a controlled chaos of coffee-stained books and papers that seemed to migrate daily, sort of like birds following some mysterious seasonal pattern.

"Mr. Harrison," Dr. Fitz said, interrupting his own lecture. "Since you seem so engaged with today's discussion, perhaps you'd like to share your thoughts on Santiago's decision to go out beyond the usual fishing grounds?"

A few people snickered. Sam looked up from his detailed rendering of a BMW airhead engine. "He went out too far because he was desperate."

"Ah." Dr. Fitz leaned against his desk, coffee mug in hand. "Desperate people make poor decisions. Is that your analysis?"

Something in his tone made Sam actually think about the question. Sam glanced down at his sketch, then back up. "No. He went out far because that's where the big fish were. Everyone else stayed close to shore because it was safer. Easier."

"And you think that makes him brave? Or foolish?"

"I think it makes him honest." The words came out before Sam had really thought them through. "He knew what he wanted, and he knew the price. Everyone else was just... pretending to fish."

The rain drummed against the windows. Dr. Fitz studied Sam for a few moments.

"Interesting." He set down his coffee. "Most people focus on Santiago's persistence, his battle with the fish. You're more interested in the decision that led him there."

"The battle only matters because of the choice," Sam

said, warming to the idea. "If he'd stayed close to shore like everyone else, there wouldn't be a story."

"No story worth telling, anyway." Dr. Fitz turned to the rest of the class. "Mr. Harrison raises an excellent point about the relationship between choice and consequence in literature. When Santiago goes beyond the usual fishing grounds—"

"I wasn't actually making a point about literature," Sam interrupted.

"No?" Dr. Fitz's eyes crinkled with amusement. "Then what were you making a point about?"

Sam thought about the college brochures piling up on his desk at home, a lot of thoughts about Ellen's early acceptance to Princeton, about his parents' careful plans for his future. And about his grandfather Gus's stories of leaving a successful law firm to become a prosecutor in New Mexico.

"Sometimes," Sam said slowly, "the safe harbor is more dangerous than the deep water."

"Because?"

"Because at least in deep water you're being honest about the risks."

Dr. Fitz nodded, like Sam had just translated a particularly difficult passage of Latin. "See me after class, Mr. Harrison." He turned back to the board. "Now, let's talk about the significance of the marlins in this context..."

Sam stayed in his seat after the bell rang, watching the other students file out into the rain. Dr. Fitz was marking papers, his red pen moving with surgical precision.

"Am I in trouble for not paying attention?" Sam asked.

"On the contrary." Fitz looked up. "That was the most attention you've paid in weeks. Though not, perhaps, to what I was teaching."

He pulled a book from his desk drawer—a worn copy of *For Whom the Bell Tolls*.

"Hemingway wrote about people making impossible choices," he said, holding out the book. "About the difference between what we're expected to do and what we know we must do. I think you might find it interesting."

"I'm not really much of a reader."

"No, you're not much for assigned reading. There's a difference." He set the book on Sam's desk. "This isn't assigned. Think of it as... research."

"Research for what?"

"That's the question, isn't it?" Dr. Fitz picked up his red pen again. "Sometimes we have to read other people's stories before we can understand our own."

Sam took the book, its cover worn smooth by other people's hands. "Is this going to help me with the test next week?"

"Probably not." He smiled. "But it might help you with something more important."

"Like what?"

"Like figuring out whether you're more afraid of the deep water or the safe harbor."

Outside, the rain had slackened to a drizzle. Sam put the book in his backpack, next to college brochures he hadn't opened and application essays he hadn't started.

"Dr. Fitz?"

"Hmm?"

"What happened to Santiago's fish in the end?"

"Read the book again," he said. "And this time, ask yourself if that's really the question that matters."

CHAPTER 2

COLLEGE

Mrs. Henderson's college counseling office felt like a shrine to success. Every wall was covered with college pennants, arranged alphabetically from Amherst to Yale, their pristine felt suggesting they'd never known actual dorm room walls. Her desk held three precisely arranged stacks of paper and a small sign that read "Your Future Starts Here!" in aggressively cheerful font. "Your test scores are... concerning," she said, flipping through Sam's file. "But we can work with this. Have you considered Radford? They have a wonderful program for students who need a bit more... structure."

Sam shifted in the hard wooden chair, trying not to look at the wall calendar where she tracked application deadlines in different colored markers. Red for early decision. Blue for regular admission. Green for rolling. It was like a rainbow of other people's choices.

"I was thinking maybe a gap year," Sam said.

Her pencil stopped moving. "Oh, Sam. That's exactly the kind of defeatist thinking we need to address." She pulled out a fresh spreadsheet. "Let's look at your extra curriculars. Lacrosse is good. Very good. But we need something more... humanitarian. Have you considered starting a charity club?"

"Two months before applications are due?"

"Initiative!" She wrote something in purple ink. "Shows leadership potential, community awareness. Now, about your essay. The prompt about overcoming challenges—I think we should focus on your asthma. Really play up the medical angle."

"I haven't had an asthma attack since freshman year."

"Details." She waved her hand dismissively. "The point is the narrative. Colleges love a good medical recovery story. Shows resilience."

Sam thought about his last conversation with Dr. Fitz, just an hour before. They had been discussing Hemingway's "The Short Happy Life of Francis Macomber" after class. "Fear," he said, rolling his ancient desk chair to the window, "is only interesting when you're honest about it. Macomber isn't brave because he kills the lion. He's brave because he finally admits what he's actually afraid of."

"Which is?"

"Read it again." He'd smiled. "And this time, pay attention to what happens right before he stops being afraid."

"Sam?" Mrs. Henderson's voice pulled me back. "Are you

listening? This is important. These decisions will shape your entire future."

"Did you ever read *The Old Man and the Sea*?" Sam asked.

She blinked, thrown by the non sequitur. "I don't see how that's relevant to your college applications."

"It's about this old guy, Santiago, who goes way out past where everyone else fishes. They all think he's crazy."

"Sam, we really need to focus. Now, about your backup schools—"

"But he goes out there because that's where the real fish are. The ones worth catching."

"I understand you're feeling overwhelmed." Her tone suggested she understood nothing of the sort. "But this is not the time for metaphors. This is the time for concrete plans. Strategy." She pulled out another color-coded sheet. "Now, if we submit to these seven safety schools..."

Sam glanced past her to the window, where autumn leaves were falling in the courtyard. He slowly turned his head to look into the hallway through the glass of the office door. Across the hall he saw Dr. Fitz in his classroom, gesturing animatedly to a group of freshmen. Even from where he was, Sam could tell he was in full flow, probably connecting some ancient text to their modern lives in ways that would make them forget they were supposed to be bored.

"Sam." Mrs. Henderson's voice had taken on the sharp edge she used with struggling students. "I need you to focus. Your parents have expressed serious concerns about your commitment to this process."

9

"Yeah," Sam said, still watching Dr. Fitz's class. "They do that."

"I've helped hundreds of students get into excellent schools. But you have to trust the process. Follow the blueprint."

The word triggered another memory from Fitz's class, which had been discussing why blueprints for real buildings have to account for how people actually live, not just how architects think they should live.

"Maybe I don't want a blueprint," Sam said, standing up. "Maybe I want to draw my own plans."

"That's not how this works." She gripped her pen tighter. "Sit down, Sam. We need to be realistic here."

"You know what I learned in Dr. Fitz's class? Sometimes the most unrealistic choice is pretending to be someone you're not."

"Dr. Fitz teaches English literature," she said, making it sound like a character flaw. "I deal with the real world. With concrete facts and deadlines. With your future."

Sam shouldered his backpack. "Maybe that's the difference. He teaches us how to think about the future. You just want us to follow a map someone else drew."

"Where are you going? We haven't finished your safety school list!"

"I think," Sam said, pausing at the door, "I need to go read Hemingway again. Figure out what I'm actually afraid of."

Sam left her sitting there among her pennants and plans,

her color-coded future that looked nothing like any life Sam wanted to live. Outside her office, the hallway was empty except for the echo of Dr. Fitz's voice carrying from his classroom, something about how the best stories often start with someone choosing the wrong path for all the right reasons.

Sam smiled, thinking about Santiago in his little boat, sailing past the point where all the safe harbors ended. Past the point where other people's maps stopped being useful.

CHAPTER 3

WINTER

Sam found Dr. Fitz in the faculty parking lot after school, wrestling with an ancient bicycle lock that had rusted shut in the Virginia winter dampness.

"Need some help?" Sam asked. "My grandfather taught me a trick with WD-40 and..."

"The lock isn't the problem," he said, still fighting with the mechanism. "The problem is my stubborn belief that it might work differently this time." The lock finally gave way with a sound like a dying hinge. "Though I suppose that's true of most things we keep doing even when we know better."

"Mrs. Henderson's office called my parents."

"Ah." He straightened up, his bad knee cracking. "I take it your discussion of alternative post-graduate plans wasn't well received?"

"She said I was throwing away my future." Sam leaned

against the bike rack. "Called it a 'rejection of reality.'"

"Whose reality?"

A group of teachers walked past, arguing about parking spaces and curriculum changes. They nodded to Fitz, who they probably saw as one of their more eccentric colleagues. Someone who taught old books to unreachable kids.

"You know what's weird?" Sam said, watching them go. "Everyone keeps talking about my future like it's this thing that already exists. Like it's already been written and I just need to follow the script."

"Sounds suspiciously like literature." Fitz smiled, then winced as his knee cracked again. "You know, when Hemingway was eighteen, he didn't go to college either. Went to Kansas City, became a reporter."

"Yeah, but that was different. That was..."

"What? More romantic? More meaningful?" He shook his head. "Every generation thinks they've arrived too late for the real adventures. That all the good quests are taken."

"This isn't about quests. It's about..." Sam hesitated, trying to find the right words. "It's about everyone being so sure they know what's best for me."

"And what do you think is best for you?"

"I don't know." Sam kicked at the bike rack. "That's kind of the point."

"Ah." Fitz finally got his bike free. "So the real problem isn't that everyone else is so certain. It's that you're not."

"Isn't that worse?"

"Only if you think certainty is the same thing as truth."

He wheeled his bike around to face Sam. "You know why I love teaching *Don Quixote* every year?"

"Because it's a classic?"

"Because it's about a man who reads too many books about how life should be, and decides to go find out how life actually is." He grinned. "Even if everyone else thinks he's crazy."

"Even if he is crazy?"

"Sometimes the crazy choice and the right choice look exactly the same." He mounted his bike with careful dignity. "Just ask your grandfather about New Mexico sometime."

Sam watched him pedal away, weaving between the last cars in the parking lot. The winter light was fading, turning the school windows into mirrors that reflected nothing but sky.

CHAPTER 4

A PLAN

The rejection letters arrived in a neat stack, each one bearing the same polite regret wrapped in different college letterheads. Sam's mom had arranged them on his desk while he was at lacrosse practice, probably thinking the careful organization would somehow soften the blow. As if the rejection from UVA would hurt less knowing Princeton had said no first.

That evening Sam wandered down the block and found his grandfather, Gus, in his garage. He was bent over one of his ancient motorcycles, his gray hair catching the last light through the dusty windows. The familiar smell of motor oil and metal hung in the air. He didn't look up when Sam entered, just continued adjusting something with a wrench that probably cost more than Sam's best pair of cleats. There were two bikes parked against the wall like a pair of patient horses: a 1964 R50/2, a 1969 R60, and another was in pieces on the workbench. All were made by BMW. There were paintings leaning against another wall—mountain scenes, motorcycles in motion, and studies of light on chrome. In the corner a half-finished manuscript sat on an old desk beside mechanical drawings and repair manuals.

Gus was retired, his small law practice closed after thirty-five years. But to Sam he seemed busier than ever— painting landscapes, writing stories, and most of all, riding. Nearly every day, he told Sam, he liked to take one of his bikes up onto the Blue Ridge Parkway where, after the ride, he returned with fresh ideas for paintings or passages for his book.

"Why do you ride so much?" Sam had asked him on more than one occasion, as he watched his grandfather change the oil, check tires, or reassemble some carburetor.

"It makes me pay attention," Gus told him. "To everything. Every moment. To cars, to animals, to the angle of the sun, the smell of rain coming, the way shadows move across the road." He tightened a bolt to some exact specification. "On a motorcycle, you can't sleepwalk through life. Every moment demands your complete presence."

"So, I guess I won't be needing those college hoodies they keep trying to sell me," Sam said, dropping onto the worn leather stool beside his workbench.

The old man grunted, still focused on the bike. "Your mother called."

"Of course she did." Sam picked up a spark plug from the workbench, turning it over in his hands. "Probably updating the family tragedy timeline. First, the breakup with Ellen, now this."

"She's worried."

"She's always worried." Sam set the spark plug down harder than necessary. "Did she tell you about one of her brilliant gap year ideas? Because apparently, that's what all the other kids do when they mess up their perfect family narrative."

Gus finally straightened up, wiping his hands on an old rag. His eyes, sharp behind his reading glasses, studied Sam with the same attention he'd just given the motorcycle's engine. "Actually, I have an idea about that."

"Let me guess—some internship at a law firm? Maybe Dad can make a call to one of his college buddies?"

"I'm riding to California in June," he said, ignoring Sam's sarcasm. "Going to visit an old friend. Thought you might want to come along."

Sam waited for the catch, the hidden lesson, the carefully planned intervention. But he just turned back to his bike, adjusting the mirror with careful precision.

"On the motorcycle?"

"Unless you'd prefer to walk."

Sam looked at the R50, its metal gleaming dully in the fading light. He saw how the white pin striping highlighted the smooth curvature of the jet black fuel tank and, of course, the unique configuration of the cylinder heads of the BMW, jutting out from the engine block like stubby little wings. He had often dreamed of it cruising down the highway.

"How long?"

"A couple of weeks. Mostly camping." Gus picked up another wrench. "I'll ride this one and you'll ride the R60," he said as he pointed to the slightly newer BMW parked against the wall. He paused before adding, "And if we complete the journey, then the bike is yours. Your call, Sam. But I need to know within the next week or two. Got to make sure both bikes are ready."

Sam thought about the summer stretching ahead of him, empty except for his mother's helpful suggestions and his dad's carefully worded disappointment. He thought about Ellen, probably ordering her books for Princeton right then, moving forward while he stood still.

And then he thought about actually owning the classic motorcycle. "The bike will be mine to keep?"

"That's what I said."

"Yeah," Sam heard himself say. "Yeah, okay."

CHAPTER 5

PARENTS

Sam's mom was doing her "casual" reading at the kitchen island when Sam came down for dinner, which meant she'd been waiting there since she got home from work. Her laptop was open to a webpage about gap year programs, the ones that cost more than actual college. His dad was still in his suit, tie loosened, scrolling through his phone while the food got cold on his plate.

"I've made a decision about the gap year," Sam said, grabbing a plate from the cabinet.

His mom's head snapped up so fast Sam thought she might hurt herself. "There's this wonderful program in Costa Rica—"

"I'm going on a motorcycle trip. With Granddad Gus." Sam scooped up some rice, waiting for his announcement to hit.

His father's phone clattered onto his plate.

"Absolutely not."

"He's going to San Francisco to visit an old friend. We'll be camping mostly." Sam sat down, deliberately casual, like this was just another dinner conversation about his latest disappointment.

"On motorcycles? Camping?" His mom's voice had that slight tremor that usually preceded a comprehensive list of potential disasters. "Gus's seventy-five years old. He has no business taking a teenager across the country on a motorcycle."

"He's seventy-two, Mom. And he probably knows as much about motorcycle maintenance as anyone in Virginia."

"This isn't about motorcycle maintenance, Sam." His dad had switched into his courtroom voice. "This is about responsibility. About making mature decisions after—"

"After screwing up my college applications?" The rice suddenly tasted like sawdust. "Because that's what this is really about, right?"

"We're trying to help you build a future," his mother said, reaching for Sam's hand. Sam pulled it back. "These gap year programs look wonderful on college applications. They show initiative, personal growth—"

"They show that you can pay thirty grand to make rich kids feel better about themselves while building houses in countries they can't find on a map."

"Watch your tone," his father warned.

"Why? Are you going to ground me from the summer I already don't have plans for?"

The silence that followed felt like the moment before a storm. His mom had that look she got when she was trying not to cry, and his dad was doing his slow head shake that meant Sam had disappointed him yet again.

"Gus put you up to this, didn't he?" his dad finally said. "This is exactly like him, making impulsive decisions without considering the consequences."

"Actually, it was my idea," Sam lied, just to see his dad's face change. "I asked him if I could go along."

"Honey," his mom tried again, "I know you're upset about Ellen, and the colleges—"

"This isn't about Ellen." Sam stood up, his chair scraping against the floor. "Or college. Or whatever else you think I'm running away from. Maybe I just want to do something that isn't part of some perfect plan for once."

"And what happens after?" His dad's voice had that dangerous calm he used when he thought he was being reasonable. "When summer's over and you've wasted months that could have been spent on your college education, or at least on some meaningful activities?"

Sam thought about Dr. Fitz's classes, and about the different books they had discussed. He thought about wars going on around the world, the corrupt and gutless politicians, the greed, the out of control capitalism, not to mention the goddam globe burning up because of climate change. He thought about Granddad Gus in his garage, planning a journey just because he could. About Ellen packing for Princeton, following the exact path she'd mapped out in ninth grade.

"Maybe that's the whole point," he said. "Maybe I need to figure out what 'meaningful' actually means. To me. Not to you, or mom, or whatever college admissions officer you're trying to impress."

"Sam—" his mom started.

"Granddad's leaving in June. I'm going with him." Sam headed for the stairs, then turned back. "And before you call him to complain, remember that I'm just about eighteen. Legally, I can make my own decisions."

"Just because you can do something legally doesn't make it wise," his dad called after him, lawyer to the end.

"Yeah, well, neither does doing something just because everyone expects you to."

Sam took his plate with him upstairs, a minor act of rebellion that felt surprisingly good. Through his bedroom wall, Sam could hear his parents start to argue in those tight, controlled voices they used when they thought he couldn't hear. His mom would call Granddad Gus that night, probably try to talk him out of it. But somehow Sam knew he wouldn't change his mind.

For the first time since the rejection letters arrived, since Ellen broke up with him, since everything started falling apart, Sam felt something like excitement. Or maybe it was just relief. Either way, it felt more real than anything had in months.

CHAPTER 6

SCHOOL ENDS

It was the last day of classes, and Sam had stayed behind, pretending to look for a nonexistent notebook while the other seniors filed out, already halfway into their summer.

"Something on your mind, Sam?" Dr. Fitz didn't look up from the essay he was marking, his red pen moving across the page like he was conducting a tiny orchestra.

"Just wondering why you never asked about my college plans." Sam responded. "Every other teacher had made it their personal mission to 'help me reach my potential,' which mostly meant suggesting safety schools with rolling admissions."

Dr. Fitz set down his pen and leaned back in his chair, which creaked in familiar protest. "Would asking have changed anything?"

Sam dropped into the front row desk he'd never actually

sat in during class, always preferring the strategic anonymity of the middle rows. "Probably not."

"Then why waste both our time?" He pulled out a worn paperback from his desk drawer and tossed it to Sam. *Don Quixote*. "Though I will say, if you'd put half the effort into your other assignments as you did analyzing *The Old Man and the Sea*, you might have had different options."

"That's because Hemingway didn't waste words trying to sound important." Sam flipped through the book's pages, dense with his familiar cramped notes in the margins. "He just told the story."

"And you think Cervantes wastes words?"

"I wouldn't know. Haven't read it."

"But you have opinions about Hemingway's style." His eyes crinkled with amusement. "You know what I liked about your essay, Sam? You wrote about the old man's failure like it meant something. Most students see it as a tragedy— the fish lost, the journey wasted. You saw it differently."

Sam shrugged, uncomfortable with the praise. "He didn't give up. That's what mattered."

"Even when everyone else thought he was crazy for going out so far?" Dr. Fitz reached for his coffee mug, found it empty. "Keep the book. My notes might help, though I suspect you'll find your own meaning."

"I don't really do summer reading."

"No, you just spend hours analyzing fishing metaphors for fun." He picked up his red pen again. "It's not assigned reading, Sam. Consider it more of a... travel guide."

"For what?"

"That's the thing about books like this. They have a way of becoming relevant exactly when you need them." He glanced at the clock. "Now get out of here. I have thirty freshman essays about *Romeo and Juliet* to grade, and they're all convinced it's a love story."

Sam stood up, sliding the book into his backpack. At the door, he hesitated. "What is it then? If not a love story?"

"Ask me again after you've read Don Quixote." He was already back to grading, but Sam caught the slight smile. "And Sam? Sometimes the smartest person in the room is the one who knows they're not the smartest person in the room."

It wasn't until Sam was halfway home that he realized Dr. Fitz had never actually answered his question about *Romeo and Juliet*. "Classic Fitz move," Sam said to himself. Half the time Sam couldn't tell if Fitz was teaching or just thinking out loud, but he was the only teacher who seemed to understand that confusion might be more valuable than certainty.

CHAPTER 7

HIGHER EDUCATION

A week before their departure, Sam found Gus in his garage, making adjustments to the bikes. The smell of motor oil and metal hung in the air, mixed with coffee from Gus's ancient percolator.

"Everyone thinks I'm just being lazy or rebellious," Sam said, sitting on the workbench. "About school, about college. Even Ellen thought that before she left for orientation."

Gus continued adjusting the valve clearance on Sam's bike, giving him space to talk.

"But I look at my classes—it's all just memorizing things for tests. Nobody asks why anything matters. In chemistry, we follow recipes like we're baking cookies. In history, we memorize dates without talking about what they mean. Even in English..." He pauses. "Except for Dr. Fitz, everyone just wants the right answers, not real questions."

The wrench clicked as Gus made another adjustment.

"And college would be different?"

"That's just it—it wouldn't. Four more years of the same thing, just more expensive. More memorizing, more tests, more doing things because that's what you're supposed to do." Sam picked up a spark plug wrench and turned it in his hands. "Dad's firm is full of people with perfect grades from perfect schools. They make great money doing work they hate, counting the days until retirement."

Gus wiped his hands on a shop rag. "What would make it worthwhile?"

"I want to understand things, not just memorize them. Like these bikes—when you teach me about them, everything connects. The engineering, the physics, the history... it all means something real." He set down the wrench. "Or like when Dr. Fitz talks about books—he shows us how they matter to real life, not just how to pass a test about them."

"And your parents don't understand this?"

"They think I'm throwing my life away because I won't follow their plan. Dad keeps talking about his law firm's internship program, mom keeps showing me business school brochures." Sam laughed without humor. "They're so busy planning my future, they never asked if it's the future I want."

Gus closed the valve cover, his movements precise and thoughtful. "You know, a wise person I knew used to say something about that. Said most people are so busy following the map they've been given, they never stop to ask who drew it, or why."

The garage grew darker as evening approached, but neither moved to turn on more lights.

"I don't know what I want to do," Sam admitted. "But I know I want it to matter. To make some kind of difference. Not just... collect degrees and paychecks until I die."

Gus nodded slowly, understanding in his eyes. "Sometimes," he said, "you have to leave the marked trail to find your own path. That's what this trip is really about, isn't it?"

Sam looked at the bikes, just about ready for their imminent departure. "Yeah," he said. "I guess it is."

"Sounds good," Gus replied as he looked out the window. "So, you up for another training ride along the Blue Ridge tomorrow?"

"Sure. See you then."

• • • • •

The late afternoon sun slanted across Nelson County as Gus and Sam turned their BMWs onto the gravel drive, returning from their Parkway ride. Solar panels glinted on the barn roof while chickens scattered at the bikes' approach.

Steve was a friend of Gus. He was riding bareback in worn jeans and a faded t-shirt, his business attire long since exchanged for farm clothes. He guided his horse alongside their parked bikes while his wife Mary emerged from the garden with a basket of tomatoes, her graying red hair escaping from a practical braid. Steve leaned forward and affectionately patted his horse's neck. "I'll be right there. I've got to exercise Red a bit more." He smiled as he gave the mare a little kick. She happily leaped forward and they cantered off together.

"Perfect timing," Mary called out. "Let's go inside. The bread's just coming out of the oven."

A Chevy Bolt sat charging near the barn, dust on its flanks suggesting recent trips to the farmers' market. The farmhouse kitchen smelled of fresh bread. Through the window, Sam watched Steve put his horse through its paces in the little paddock adjacent to the barn with the casual confidence of someone who rode daily, not just for show.

"Most people think you have to choose," Mary said, following Sam's gaze as she entered with Gus. "City or country, technology or tradition, business or environment. We decided that was a false choice."

The small farm was a study in contrasts—the Bolt's charging station next to the sheep pasture, sophisticated weather monitoring equipment beside the heritage vegetable garden, solar inverters sharing barn space with saddles and hay.

"Steve likes to ride every morning before work," Mary explained, slicing bread. "I do the chores, then work on correcting math papers for my engineering students. The chickens don't care if I'm thinking about differential equations while I feed them."

Later, riding home in the gathering dusk, Gus pulled alongside Sam at a stoplight.

"It's always a good idea to see how other people make

their choices," he said. "Steve and Mary found their own way—not what anyone expected from a scientist and a mathematician."

"They seem happy," Sam observed.

"That's because they didn't let others define success for them. They gathered information, saw different possibilities, then made their own choices." The light turned green. "The more you see what other people do and how they live, the better equipped you are to choose your own path."

Sam thought about this as they rode home—about a scientist or businessman who rides bareback, math professors who grew tomatoes, and how peoples' choices after school, sometimes looked like finding your own way to live with your own truth.

CHAPTER 8

PREPARATION

Gus's garage was organized chaos in the weeks before their departure. Maps spread across his workbench, camping gear sorted into neat piles, tools laid out with surgical precision. Sam noticed how his grandfather approached the preparation like he used to prepare for trials—methodical, thorough, leaving nothing to chance.

In preparation for their long ride, they often rode along the Blue Ridge Parkway, a mere twenty miles from town. Sam's 'ride' was the fifty-five year old R60/2. As they sat at the entrance gate in Afton, it idled beneath Sam like a living thing, its boxer engine rocking gently. Gus had decided to use the vintage bikes for the journey, older and simpler than the more modern touring machines.

"Feel that?" Gus asked. "How the whole bike moves with the engine? Old-timers called these 'gentleman's express' bikes, but they're really mechanical horses."

Sam understood as soon as they began to ride. The bike responded to weight shifts like a horse to leg pressure. Lean slightly, and it turned. Sit back, it settled. Press forward, it eagerly took up the pace. The sprung seat even moved like a saddle, floating over imperfections in the road.

"Watch how it tells you what it needs," Gus's voice came through the intercom. "When to feed it gas and when to ease off."

The old BMW's transmission whined in second and third gears, when climbing a hill. No modern soundproofing muffled the machinery's voice. Every component spoke directly to the rider—the engine's effort through the frame, the tires' grip through the handlebars, the transmission's mood through the shift lever.

"These old bikes, they're like trail horses," Gus explained during a rest stop. "Not the fastest, not the flashiest, but they know their job and they'll work all day if you treat them right. Listen to what they're telling you, respect their quirks, and they'll carry you anywhere."

"You know why I love these old airheads?" Gus asked as they prepared to mount up again. "Because they remind us that travel isn't just about getting somewhere. It's about the partnership between rider and mount, travelling different roads through the landscape."

The engine caught on the first kick, settling into its steady idle-rock, ready for another day's journey. Like a well-trained steed, it waited patiently for its rider's signal to begin. Sam grew to enjoy the solid-sounding 'clunk' in the gearbox when he pulled in the clutch and engaged first gear, as well as the slow, deliberate changing of its gears with his left foot as they took off.

Sam remembered seeing one of Dr. Fitz's highlighted passages in *Don Quixote* when he first got the book from him, describing Rocinante: *Though he had more corners than a quarter and more defects than Gonella's horse, which was all skin and bones, he appeared to him finer than the Bucephalus of Alexander or the Babieca of the Cid.*

The old motorcycle beneath him shared something with that ancient steed—not the fastest, not the prettiest, but faithful in its own way. Like Rocinante, the bike has its quirks and demands: the gentle choke needed on cold mornings, the careful warm-up before serious riding, the way it needed to be understood rather than merely driven.

At a rest stop Sam joked about something he had read in one of Gus's motorcycle magazines. "Well, I like these old bikes despite their flaws, you know the useless old drum brakes, bad handling, and lack of power," before adding,"- Maybe because of them."

Gus nodded, checking the bike's oil level with practiced care. "That's the thing about old machines. Their imperfections become part of their character. You don't just ride them—you form a partnership." They mounted up again, the engines settled into their steady rhythm, carrying them forward like faithful steeds into whatever adventures awaited.

Back at his garage Gus made an announcement, "Two weeks on the road," he said, checking items off his list. "We need to be self-sufficient." He had taught Sam how to pack the BMW's saddlebags efficiently—heavy items low and forward, frequently needed items easily accessible.

They had spent two evenings testing camping gear in Gus's backyard. "No surprises on the road," he insisted, showing Sam how to set up the tents quickly as darkness fell. They practiced their routine until it became almost muscle memory.

The bikes received equally thorough attention. Oil changes, valve adjustments, new tires. "These old airheads will run forever if you treat them right," Gus repeated, when he taught Sam how to check the boxer engine's valve clearances. "Like most everything—it works if you do the work."

Sam's mother kept appearing with new items she insisted they needed—first aid supplies, emergency blankets, extra batteries. His father watched from a distance, disapproving but silent, while Gus quietly added the useful items to their kit and discretely set aside the unnecessary ones.

They bought their last supplies at the camping store—freeze-dried meals, water purification tablets, repair kits. Gus insisted on redundancy for crucial items: two ways to make fire, two ways to purify water, two ways to navigate.

Below the bikes, their tools and supplies were laid out: camping gear, maps, repair kits, spare parts. Gus moved between them like a lawyer organizing exhibits, each item part of a larger argument for the jury.

"Look here," Sam said, finding another highlighted passage in Fitz's book he pulled from his backpack. He read it aloud: "*Take with thee supplies for the journey, and take also thy sword and crossbow.*" Even Don Quixote's niece knew you don't start a quest without proper equipment."

They worked through their own preparations:

- Weather gear sorted by climate zones
- First aid supplies double-checked
- Emergency contacts listed
- Routes mapped with alternatives
- Camping gear tested and verified
- Tools organized for quick access
- Spare parts cataloged and stored

"You know what my boss used to say?" Gus asked, adjusting Sam's new throttle cable. "'Cases are won in preparation, not performance.' Same with journeys like this."

The bikes gleamed under the garage lights, ready for their quest. Like Don Quixote's armor, they've been polished and prepared, every part checked, every system verified. Not just machines anymore, but companions for the journey ahead.

"Here's another one," Sam said laughingly, finding his place in the paperback: "*The wise man is prepared for anything; the fool only for what he hopes will happen.*"

"So true," Gus said, adding another package of waterproof matches to their kit.

Two nights before departure, they were doing a final check of everything. Sam noticed how each item had its place, how the packing had its own kind of poetry. In his backpack, *Don Quixote* waited in both its paperback and audio book form, ready to accompany their journey west.

"Ready?" Gus asked, looking at their loaded bikes gleaming in the garage light.

Sam thought about the miles ahead, about all the preparation, about how the journey begins long before the first mile.

"Ready," he said, and meant it.

CHAPTER 9

DEPARTURE

The morning Sam and Gus left, mist hung in the Shenandoah Valley like something from a dream. Sam had barely slept, lying awake listening to the house settle and his parents argue in low voices downstairs. Sam stood in the driveway, watching Gus do his final check on each of the bikes while his mother hovered nearby with a list of emergency contacts.

"I've programmed all the hospital locations along your route into your phone," she said, handing Sam a printout. "And I packed extra antihistamines in case you have an allergic reaction to... well, anything."

"Thanks, Mom." Sam tucked the paper into his jacket without looking at it.

His father stood off to the side, arms crossed, still wearing his workout clothes from his morning run. He hadn't said much since their argument about the trip, like he was saving his words for some future courtroom where he could prove he'd been right all along.

"Oil level's good," Gus announced, standing up from his inspection. "Weather looks generally clear to Louisville." He glanced at his son. "David, you want to check my work? Make sure I haven't missed anything?"

His jaw tightened. "I'm sure you know what you're doing."

"Usually." Gus smiled.

The sun was starting to burn through the mist, revealing a perfect June morning. Down the street, Sam could see Ellen's house, her driveway empty since she'd left for Princeton's early orientation program. The sight didn't hurt as much as he'd expected.

"Sam?" His mom's voice had that tremor again. "You can still change your mind. There's still time to…"

"To what?" Sam asked. "Apply to safety schools? Start a charity club?"

"To make sensible choices," his dad cut in. "To think about your future."

Sam looked at the bikes gleaming in the morning light. At the camping gear strapped to the back, the miles of road ahead, the stories waiting to be told. At his grandfather, who'd once chosen an impossible quest over a safe harbor.

"Maybe that's what I'm doing," Sam said, putting on his helmet.

He had even brought Dr. Fitz's copy of *Don Quixote*, along with the audiobook loaded on his phone, something that Gus had been pleasantly surprised to hear about. He told Sam it was one of his favorite books and that he had read it cover to cover. "Some say the book has been so popular over the centuries because back then, in the 1600s, people would sit around and have these wild adventures of Don Quixote read to them. It was all about entertainment, like watching a comedy series on TV before they had TVs and iPhones." He shook his head. "It's probably why the most successful politicians these days come from the entertainment industry." He paused. "Personally, I interpret the story differently."

With that, Gus mounted his bike. The engine started with a muffled roar and quickly settled into a quiet rumble. Sam kick started his bike and swung his leg over the saddle. After completing the motorcycle safety course, securing his motorcycle license, and taking a few practice rides, he felt the familiar vibration and grinned. The whole machine seemed to lean forward, eager for motion. "Sam?" Sam looked at his mom, who was trying not to cry. "Just... be careful."

"I will," Sam replied with a smile. "But maybe not too careful."

The pair pulled out of the driveway. In the mirror, Sam could see his parents growing smaller, becoming figures in a story he was riding away from. The morning sun caught a chrome piece of Gus's bike, making it flash like a signal to some distant watchman.

Just before they turned onto the main road, Sam saw Dr. Fitz on his bicycle, headed to school for the summer session, early like always. He raised his travel coffee mug in salute as the motorcycles passed, and Sam remembered what he'd said about stories starting with the wrong choice for the right reasons.

The mist had burned away and revealed a sky so blue it almost hurt to look at. Ahead of them, the road unwound like a story waiting to be read. Or maybe written. Sam wasn't sure which yet, but for the first time in a long time, the uncertainty felt like freedom.

CHAPTER 10

VIRGINIA TO KENTUCKY

The BMW's boxer engine thrummed beneath them as they left the interstate behind, turning onto Virginia Route 250. The road followed the contours of the land instead of cutting through it, rolling with the valley's natural rhythm. The morning mist still clung to some of the hollows while the Shenandoah Valley spread out around them.

Gus lead them through a landscape of family farms and small towns, the old R50's fairing parting the cool morning air. These roads demanded attention—blind curves, sudden drops, the occasional gravel wash across a corner. The ancient BMWs responded to every input, their air-cooled engines talking back through the frame, through the handlebars, through the seat.

"Listen to her breathing," Gus's voice came through the intercom as they climbed toward a mountain gap. The bikes' exhausts echoed off a rock cut, while the engines pulled steadily in second and third gear. "These old airheads love mountain roads. They were built for the Alps."

Over Afton Mountain and through Waynesboro, where the factories stood quiet in the early light, the bikes' air-cooled engines worked steadily on the climbs, their exhausts echoing off the rock cuts. West of Staunton, the valley opened up, rolling farmland stretched toward distant ridges. They passed through Churchville, West Augusta, McDowell—towns that seemed to exist in defiance of time's passage. Each had its own character: a proud courthouse square, a row of brick storefronts with hand-painted signs, grain silos standing like sentinels.

"Watch how the architecture changes," Gus's voice came through the intercom as they crossed into Highland County. "Virginia brick giving way to Kentucky limestone."

They stopped for fuel in Monterey, where the gas station doubled as the town's gathering spot. Old men in chairs outside the convenience store watched them check their oil levels and adjust their loads.

Through West Virginia's narrow slice, the roads became more dramatic—tight curves and sudden grades that made the old bikes earn their keep. Small coal towns appeared and vanished, their company stores now antique shops, their rail lines quiet.

Crossing into Kentucky, the landscape changed but the roads kept their character. Route 68 took them through tobacco country, past weathered barns with faded Mail

Pouch ads on their sides. The bikes settled into a rhythm—fourth gear through the valleys, third for the climbs, the occasional shift to second on really steep inclines.

"Feel how the frame talks to you?" Gus asked during a rest stop. "These old bikes, they tell you everything—about the road, about their needs, about what's coming next. You just have to learn their language."

Sam nodded, understanding why his grandfather loved these old machines. They were not just transportation—they were companions, teaching a slower, more attentive way of moving through the world. Each mile brought new conversations between rider and machine, between present and past, between the road ahead and the story unfolding beneath their wheels.

Kentucky arrived with subtle changes—different styles of barns, tobacco instead of hay, limestone fences marking old property lines. They rode through Paris, Georgetown, Frankfort, each town offered its own glimpse of America in transition.

Hours later the Appalachians finally released their grip on the pair somewhere in eastern Kentucky, and the tight mountain curves gave way to rolling hills that stretched endlessly under a hazed summer sky. The two had been riding all day, and the landscape changed from Virginia's dense green forests to farmland that rippled like waves in the late afternoon light. Sam's legs felt like they'd forgotten how to work, and the June sun baked him inside his motorcycle jacket. He had listened to music through his earphones for most of the day and then, at an afternoon gas stop, decided to switch to his audio book of *Don Quixote*. The narrator's voice was still echoing in his head and it was working as a pretty good distraction from the long hours of riding.

Gus led the two of them off the highway just outside Louisville, taking a winding road that cut through fields of corn just tall enough to create low walls on either side of the pavement. The camping spot he chose was at the Taylorsville Lake State Park, which sat at the edge of a small lake, where fat carp occasionally broke the surface, sending ripples across water that reflected the orange-purple sunset. The air smelled different there—cleaner, with hints of wild honeysuckle and sun-warmed earth.

After parking the motorcycles at their camp site, Gus moved with the ease of someone who'd done this a hundred times, unpacking his saddlebags with practiced efficiency. Behind him, a freight train crawled along a distant track, its whistle echoing across the farmland. Sam tried to mirror his grandfather's movements, but failed miserably at rolling out his sleeping bag.

"Your father called," Gus said, arranging kindling for a fire. A bird, Sam thought maybe a whip-poor-will, schrieked from somewhere in the darkness gathering under the trees. "Three times."

"Let me guess—he wanted to remind you about your responsibility to deliver me back unbroken."

"Actually, he wanted to make sure you had your inhaler." Gus struck a match, nurturing the small flame with patience.

"Which I do, by the way. Your mother packed two."

Sam hadn't needed an inhaler since ninth grade, but he didn't say that. Instead, he watched the fire catch, thinking about how different the flame looked out in the woods than it did in his parents' carefully screened fireplace. Here, it seemed alive, dancing with the evening breeze that rustled through the trees.

A few minutes passed and Sam looked over at his grandfather. "I started listening to *Don Quixote* this afternoon on my audiobook. Just before we left you said you really liked it. Is that true? I mean, when did you read it?"

Gus thought for a minute. "I remember Mrs. Peterson's World Literature class. It was my junior year, fifth period, right after lunch when everyone was half asleep. She'd reduced *Don Quixote* to bullet points on the blackboard. It went something like this: It was a comic novel about a delusional old man who thought he was a knight and went on imaginary adventures. I remember she told us it was the source of the word 'quixotic,' which meant foolishly idealistic." He paused to think and then added, "Oh yeah, and it was written to entertain Spanish readers and basically mocked the outdated chivalric romances of the time."

Gus continued. "I was barely paying attention, mostly doodling motorcycles in my notebook while she explained how the book was just an elaborate joke, a way to mock people who took old stories too seriously. I remember we spent one day on it, then moved on to more 'important" works.'"

"So you read it in high school?"

"It's a very long book and I basically skimmed it for that class. After college I really read it."

Sam nodded and poked the fire so it crackled and sent sparks upward.

"I discovered that she had it all wrong," Gus said suddenly. "In class, she taught us it was just entertainment. Just stories about a crazy old man who couldn't tell reality from fantasy."

Sam looked up from the fire. "And now?"

"I'm not sure what's crazier—seeing giants where everyone else sees windmills, or seeing windmills when you know they're really giants."

Sam waited silently for more. Hearing none, he asked, "So, who's Phil?"

Gus sat back on his heels, the firelight catching the silver in his hair. Behind him, the last light was fading from the sky, turning the lake to a polished glass. "What makes you ask about Phil?"

"Mom said that's who we're going to see. She said he was your boss in New Mexico or something."

"He was more than my boss." Gus pulled out a battered camping kettle. The metal had the patina of countless fires, countless conversations. "Want some coffee?"

"It's eight at night."

"Best time for coffee." He filled the kettle from his water bottle. "Phillip Stone was... imagine meeting Don Quixote in real life."

A chorus of cicadas had started up in the darkness, their

thrumming a constant backdrop to the conversation. Heat lightning flickered silently on the horizon, illuminating the tower of clouds that looked like some distant mountains.

"The guy who thought he was a knight and went on crazy adventures?" Sam had only gotten through the first few chapters on the day's ride, the words mixing with the rhythm of the motorcycle and the changing landscape. He remembered that Don Quixote was accompanied by a befuddled laborer named Sancho Panza and that he rode an old nag workhorse named Rocinante.

"Wasn't he sort of off his rocker and causing trouble wherever he went?"

Gus laughed, but it wasn't his usual laugh. It carried something else, something Sam couldn't quite name. "That's what everyone said about Phil, too. At first." He set the kettle over the fire. "Back in the mid-nineteen eighties, he was head of the criminal prosecutions division for the Attorney General in New Mexico. I was fresh out of law school, and thought I knew everything."

The kettle started to whistle, its sound competing with the night insects and the occasional splash of jumping fish. Gus pulled out two enamel cups that looked older than Sam, their blue coating chipped to reveal silver beneath. The stars appeared in the darkening sky above them.

A log popped in the fire, sending sparks up to join the fireflies that had begun to emerge from the surrounding cornfields. In the distance, a truck's horn echoed off the highway, although it felt like it was coming from another world entirely.

The air had cooled enough to raise goosebumps on Sam's arms, carrying the scent of wood smoke and approaching rain.

"So, why did you become a lawyer in the first place?" Sam asked. "I mean, how did you know that was what you wanted to do?"

Gus smiled. "I didn't." He looked at Sam. "In a lot of ways, I was just like you. I didn't know what to do after I got through high school so I took a year off."

"Really? What did you do? I mean you must have gone to college to get into law school, right?"

"Well, after working as a cook and then in a bike shop for a year, I figured that I would rather do a less labor intensive job and decided to get a college degree. So, I went to the local college, got my diploma and then taught at a junior high school for a couple of years." Gus chuckled. "That was quite an experience."

"Yeah, I can imagine. Did you like it?"

"I liked working with the kids, for sure. After a couple of years I felt pressure to do something else, to push myself."

"Yeah, I remember those junior high school years. I remember I was mostly bored." Sam said.

Gus went on. "As I recall, in junior high and through high school it was really important to me to be part of the group. I took up sports, which helped a lot, being part of a team."

Sam nodded. "To be honest, that was pretty hard for me. I got pretty stressed out when I started to fall behind in my classwork and I wasn't too athletic either, mostly on the backup squad." Sam asked, "So, was law school really hard? And how did you know you wanted to be a lawyer?

"If you want to know, I hated law school, especially the first year. It was so intimidating and that Socratic method of teaching was brutal."

"My dad talked about that," Sam replied. "That's where the teacher points to you and grills you in front of the whole class, right?"

"That's right." Gus paused for a second before he continued. "Even though I had gone through college and was an older student, I always cringed at the idea of being humiliated, especially in front of a large group of people. And then, in law school it happened. You never knew when you would be called on, and the professors seemed to enjoy putting you on the spot. Quite honestly, it was very rough for me."

"Yeah, I know what you mean," Sam said. "There's nothing worse than getting put down in public. So, when did you finally get over it, that feeling of getting panicky under pressure?"

"Well, now that I think of it, I probably never have. They say there's nothing wrong with feeling stress under pressure. That everyone experiences it and it's perfectly normal. But, I'd say I finally got over the performance anxiety as a lawyer when I started working as a prosecutor in New Mexico and doing a bunch of court cases."

"Really? How did that all happen?"

"After law school your grandmother Anne and I moved to Santa Fe and both had jobs as lawyers. She worked at the big law firm in town and I worked for a small law firm, which

I didn't much like. I then went to work at the district attorney's office, prosecuting street crime cases." Gus paused as he recalled his early days. "That's when I first met Phil Stone. I was on a break and wandered into this courtroom and a jury trial was going on. It was a fraud case and I was struck by what I saw." He stopped and smiled. "It was like watching a musical performance. The prosecutor was up in front of the jury, displaying exhibits, making objections, cross examining witnesses, and then finished with a captivating closing argument. Anyway, I don't want to bore you with all these legal terms, but let me just say there was a beautiful rhythm to what he was doing. After watching him in action, I knew I wanted to work for him."

"And I guess you did, right? And I presume that was the Phil I've heard about?"

"That's right. Phil became not only my boss, but my mentor and good friend. A few years later your grandmother and I moved to Virginia to be closer to our families. I was a prosecutor for a few years and then started my own law practice as a defense attorney." Gus smiled. "Over the years, whenever I had a big case going to trial, I would call Phil up to talk strategy. He never hesitated to drop whatever he was doing to talk and give me advice."

"So, I always wondered why you become a defense attorney? I mean, I can see being a prosecutor and putting bad guys in jail, but how could you defend guilty people?"

Gus poked at the fire thoughtfully. "Think of it like a balance scale. Justice isn't just about putting people in jail.

It's about making sure the system works fairly for everyone."

"But as a prosecutor, you were fighting for what's right."

"As a defense attorney, I was still fighting for what's right—just in a different way." Gus set down his coffee cup. "The system only works if both sides do their jobs properly. Prosecutors represent the state, which means the people who live in a particular place, and work to pursue justice on behalf of society. But defense attorneys protect individual rights, to make sure the government proves its case, and to prevent abuse of power."

Sam watched the fire flicker. "Even when your client is guilty?"

"Yes. It's important to remember that every person accused of a crime has constitutional rights. If we let those rights erode for guilty people, they'll eventually erode for innocent ones too." He looked at Sam. "When I defended someone, I was not just defending that person—I was defending the principles that protect everyone's rights."

"But what about truth? Justice?"

"Truth emerges from the process, which in the criminal justice system is adversarial."

"What does that mean?" Sam asked.

"Here's how it works," Gus explained. "The prosecution presents its evidence, defense tests that evidence, challenges assumptions, ensures proper procedure. The judge referees, and the jury decides what's true." Gus added another log to the fire. "Without strong defense attorneys, the system becomes unbalanced. Power goes unchecked. Innocent people get crushed."

Sam considered this point as the stars emerged above them. "I think I get it," he said. "That's sounds pretty cool. So what kind of advice would he give you?" Sam wanted to know.

"What?"

"Phil. You were talking about your friend. What kind of advice would Phil give you."

"Oh yeah," Gus nodded. "We would come up with different strategies on how to win the case. It was serious business, but we would still joke around and have fun at the same time. Humor helped to ease the tension. I guess it mostly came down to connecting with a friend and confidant. And, of course, figuring out how to tell a captivating story about good deeds and justice in a stacked legal system."

Sam thought of the Don Quixote story he had been listening to that afternoon. "So, is that what you were?" Sam asked. "Phil's Sancho Panza?"

Gus smiled, but his eyes stayed on the fire. "Maybe that's what this trip is about. Figuring out who played what part in the real story."

"What story?"

"Get some sleep, Sam. We've got a long ride tomorrow, and I want to show you something when we get to New Mexico." He poured the rest of his coffee into the fire, which hissed in protest. "Something about giants and windmills."

Sam wanted to press him further, but there was something in his voice that suggested the conversation was over. At least for the time being. Sam settled into his sleeping bag, listening to the fire crack and pop and the cicadas singing their endless song. The heat lightning was closer and illuminated the undersides of clouds which promised the next day would bring different weather, different landscapes, and different stories.

Just before he drifted off, Sam heard his grandfather say quietly, "You know, your father never asked me about Phil."

But when Sam lifted his head to respond, Gus was already in his own sleeping bag, back turned to the dying fire. Above the pair, the stars were indifferent to the stories being told beneath them.

CHAPTER 11

KENTUCKY TO MISSOURI

They broke camp at dawn, dew heavy on the tents and the whip-poor-wills still singing their last songs. The Kentucky air was thick with humidity, and Sam could feel it building as they packed. Once underway, in Sam's helmet, Don Quixote was explaining his quest to a bewildered innkeeper, the words nearly lost under the thrum of the BMW's boxer engine.

Know, good sir, that my profession requires that I wander the world righting wrongs and redressing injuries. I cannot, therefore, be concerned with my own comfort when duty calls me to face perils that promise glory. For what greater purpose might a knight have than to bring justice where there is cruelty, aid where there is need, and truth where there are lies? Though you may look upon me with doubt, history shall record my deeds among those who fought for righteousness when others sought merely their own ease.

They took Kentucky Route 44 west, the old bikes rumbling through towns where tobacco barns were giving way to suburban development. Through Mount Washington, where weekend farmers' trucks mixed with commuters heading toward Louisville.

"Watch the humidity," Gus warned through the intercom. "These old airheads run rich when the air gets thick." Sam nodded. He had learned that the carburetors sat next to the cylinder heads and fed a gas vapor into the cylinders and caused the explosion ignited by the spark plugs, pushing the pistons up and down to spin the crankshaft, but he knew that it would be his grandfather who actually made any of the gas-to-air ratio adjustments.

It then happened in an instant. As they were riding through a wooded stretch in western Kentucky, the afternoon sun created dappled shadows across the road. A flash of movement from the right, and suddenly a young deer bound across the pavement directly into Sam's path.

No time to brake. No time to swerve. The deer hit the front fender of Sam's bike with a sickening thud, its body glancing off as it tumbled to the roadside. The impact bent the fender back against the tire, the metal scraping with each rotation.

"Hold steady!" Gus's voice cut through the intercom. "Don't brake hard, just ease off the throttle."

Sam fought his instinct to jam on the brakes as he felt the bike wobble beneath him. His heart hammered in his chest as he managed to slow gradually, keeping the machine upright despite the drag from the damaged fender. They pulled onto the shoulder and the bikes came to a stop on the gravel.

Gus was off his bike instantly, moving to check Sam first, then the machine. "You okay?"

Sam nodded, his hands shaking as he removed his helmet. "Is the deer...?"

They looked back to see the young buck stagger to its feet, seemingly dazed but alive. It disappeared into the woods with a halting gait.

"Lucky for both of you," Gus said, turning his attention to the bike. The front fender was pushed up against the tire, preventing it from turning freely. Gus pulled tools from his saddlebag with practiced efficiency and loosened the fender mounts.

"Hold the handlebars straight," he instructed. Using a large screwdriver as a lever, he pried the bent metal away from the tire. A few more adjustments and the wheel turned freely again.

"We'll need to check it out more completely when we stop for the night," Gus said as he tightened the remaining bolts. "But this will get us to the campground."

Sam's hands have finally stopped shaking. "I didn't even see it coming."

"Nobody ever does." Gus patted his shoulder. "But you didn't panic and kept the bike up. That's what matters."

They mounted up again and continued on, more cautiously. The encounter had shaken something loose in

Sam—a reminder of how quickly circumstances can change, how thin the margin is between control and chaos. The damaged bike carried them forward, a little bent but still running, much like its rider.

They crossed the Ohio River at Louisville, the bridges carrying them into Indiana where the landscape flattened and broadened. Through Corydon, with its limestone courthouse and memories of being Indiana's first capital. The air grew heavier as they pushed west, thunderheads building in the distance.

Small towns appeared with rhythmic regularity—Salem, Paoli, French Lick with its grand old resort hotels. Each had its own personality: a restored downtown square, a proud water tower, grain elevators marking the skyline like medieval castles.

They crossed Illinois on the secondary roads, and Sam noticed that the farms grew larger, more industrial. The prairie began to assert itself—subtle at first, then unmistakable in its vastness. Through towns like Flora, Salem, and Centralia, where coal country met corn country.

"Different kind of wealth here," Gus noted during a gas stop. "Measured in acres instead of square feet."

The Mississippi River appeared as a silver ribbon on the horizon. They crossed at Chester, Illinois, the river marked more than just a state line—it was a threshold into the true Midwest. Missouri spread before them, the Ozark hills promising curves after the prairie's straight lines.

Through Farmington with its lead mining history,

Potosi with its century-old courthouse, and Rolla, where the university brought youth to an old mining town. The humidity built as they neared the Lake of the Ozarks, the air thick enough to feel like something solid.

Gus took them on a detour west of St. Louis. They pulled off Route 66 near what was once Times Beach, Missouri. It was renamed Route 66 State Park, but Gus remembered its darker history. They parked their bikes and walked to an overlook above the Meramec River.

"This whole area used to be a town," Gus said as he gestured at the empty parkland. "Times Beach. Two thousand people lived here until 1983. Now it's a ghost town, abandoned because of dioxin contamination."

Sam looked across the seemingly peaceful landscape. "What happened?"

"It was one of the worst environmental disasters in the nation's history. Started in 1971. Local waste hauler, Russell Bliss, was paid to spray oil on dirt roads to keep the dust down. Looked like he was doing the town a favor—free service." Gus's voice carried the weight of the remembered event. "Turned out he was mixing waste oil with industrial byproducts containing TCDD—one of the most toxic forms of dioxin."

They walked along a trail, the summer breeze carried no hint of the poison that once saturated the soil.

"The same oil had killed horses at a local stable, but nobody made the connection at first. People's pets started dying. Kids got sick. But the spraying continued for years."

Gus stopped at an interpretive sign. "When the truth finally came out, the EPA had to evacuate the entire town. The federal government spent $250 million buying out properties and cleaning up the contamination."

"Did anyone go to prison?"

"Bliss claimed he didn't know the oil was toxic. The chemical companies that produced the waste claimed they weren't responsible for what happened to it afterward." Gus shook his head. "Same pattern with the energy companies—profit from the damage, deny the consequences, let others pay the price."

They stood in silence, watching the river flow past.

"You know what Phil would say about this place?" Gus finally spoke. "He'd say it's not just a cautionary tale about environmental disaster. It's a story about how truth takes time to emerge, about how corporate responsibility gets buried like toxic waste, waiting for someone brave enough to dig it up."

Back on their bikes, Sam looked again at the empty parkland that used to be Times Beach, and he understood a little more about why some battles needed to be fought, even when the foe seemed too big to defeat.

Gus led them west on back roads that wound through tobacco fields and horse farms. The morning unfolded in a rhythm of curves and straightaways, the landscape had changed from Kentucky's manicured pastures to Missouri's wilder hills. By noon, the humidity had become something physical, pressing against them like an actual wall.

"Weather's building," Gus's voice came through the intercom installed in their helmets. "Watch the clouds to the southwest."

Sam saw them—thunderheads stacking up like towers, their tops spreading out in anvil shapes against the blue. The air took on a metallic taste that precedes summer storms, and the temperature dropped suddenly.

The storm caught them halfway across Missouri. In Sam's helmet, before the intercom crackled with weather static, Don Quixote spoke of such moments: *For knights-errant take pride in being tormented by the weather, since the hardships they endure demonstrate their courage to all who witness them.*

They had been watching the storm build for hours—thunderheads stacking up like mountains in the western sky, the air growing thick with electricity. The wind soon picked up, buffeting their bikes across the two-lane highway.

"Weather's coming," Gus's voice broke through. "Remember what I told you. Smooth inputs. Let the bike find its balance."

The first drops hit like bullets. Within minutes, the rain was torrential. Their old BMWs plowed through standing water, the airhead engines steady despite the deluge. Lightning split the sky, followed instantly by thunder that shook the air around them.

Through his rain-streaked visor, Sam recalled another line from the audio book: "*Let us press on, for a knight must endure hardship and foul weather with a stout heart, taking them as signs that greater glory awaits.*" The words seem fitting as he watched Gus's taillight weave slightly against the crosswinds.

"Don't fight the bike," Gus reminded him. "She knows how to handle this."

Water pooled in their boots and ran down their necks despite their rain gear. But the motorbikes kept moving, their ancient engines unfazed by the storm. Each flash of lightning revealed a landscape transformed—fields turned to lakes, trees bending in the wind, roads became rivers.

They found shelter under an abandoned gas station's canopy, the bikes' engines ticking as they cooled. Steam rose from the hot cylinders as the rain drummed on the metal roof above.

"These old airheads," Gus said, removing his helmet, "they're at their best when things are worst. Like they enjoy showing you what they're made of."

"Like Rocinante," Sam added, thinking of Don Quixote's faithful steed facing countless storms and trials.

"Exactly," Gus nodded. "The book gets it right—there's honor in enduring hardship, in pressing forward when others seek shelter."

The rain continued its percussion on the roof while they waited, the bikes dripping quietly, like faithful steeds resting between adventures, ready to carry them onward when the storm passes.

After the rain let up, the two rode on to a small town called Cedar Grove. Gus signaled right, leading them down a main street that looked preserved from the 1950s. They parked under the awning of Mae's Diner just as the sky opened up again.

Inside, the air conditioning hit them like an artic blast. The place smelled of coffee and pie and years of grilled onions. Their gear dripped on the checkered floor as a waitress named Ruby brought them menus and sympathy.

"You boys picked the right time to stop," she said, pouring coffee without asking. "These storms mean business."

Thunder punctuated her words, and rain drummed against the windows. Sam watched lightning sketch white lines between earth and sky while Gus ordered pie for both of them.

"Long way from home," Ruby said, noticing their Virginia plates through the window. "Where you headed?"

"California," Gus told her. "Going to visit an old friend."

"Must be some friend."

Gus's smile carried something Sam hadn't seen before. "He is. We worked together in New Mexico, years ago. Prosecutor's office in Santa Fe."

It's the first time Sam had heard Gus mention Phil to a stranger. Something in his voice made Sam pay closer attention.

"Prosecutors?" Ruby topped off their coffee. "Like putting bad guys in jail?"

"Sometimes," Gus said. "Sometimes just trying to make powerful people tell the truth."

Lightning flashed again, and in that instant, Sam saw

something cross his grandfather's face—a memory or a regret, he was not sure which.

"Hard work, I expect," Ruby said.

"The hardest part wasn't finding the truth," Gus replied. "It was getting people to see it once we found it."

The storm moved east, taking its fury but leaving the sky unsettled. They finished their pie while Gus told Ruby about the New Mexico light and desert air.

Back on the bikes, the world felt washed clean. Sam passed the hours of riding by listening to music or the Don Quixote story. The late afternoon sun broke through beneath the clouds, turning everything to gold and copper. The air smelled of rain-soaked earth and distant lightning.

The approach to Lake of the Ozarks took them through rolling hills that reminded Sam of waves that got frozen in mid-motion. The lake appeared through gaps in the trees, each glimpse bigger than the last, until finally they rounded a bend and the whole expanse opened up before them.

They made camp on a point overlooking the water. The sunset turned the lake to a big orange flame, and leftover clouds caught fire in the dying light. Sam helped Gus set up the tents, their movements having become more practiced with each stop.

"Your friend from New Mexico," Sam said as they sat watching the sky grow dark. "The one we're going to see in San Francisco. Tell me more about him."

Gus was quiet for a long moment, poking at their small campfire with a stick. Around them, the darkness was filling up with insect songs and the soft lapping of water against the shore.

"Phil," Gus finally said. "saw things other people couldn't. Or wouldn't." He looked up at Sam. "Kind of like your Don Quixote."

"What kind of things?"

"That's a longer story." Gus added another stick to the fire. "One that needs the right landscape to tell it properly."

The sun made its final bow, setting the western clouds ablaze. In the distance, heat lightning flickered between earth and sky, like signals being passed between hidden conspirators.

"When will we reach the right landscape?" Sam asked.

"Soon enough," Gus said. "When the trees thin out and the sky opens up."

Sam thought about Ruby in the diner, about the way Gus's voice changed when he mentioned New Mexico. About truth and power and stories that needed the right setting to be told.

In his pocket, his phone was paused on Don Quixote's explanation of knight-errantry, of searching for adventures and righting wrongs. Above them, the first stars appeared between the clouds, while all around, the darkness filled with possibility and questions waiting to be asked.

CHAPTER 12

MISSOURI TO KANSAS

They left Lake of the Ozarks in early morning light. The old motorcycles climbed out of the lake region through twisting roads that slowly straightened as the Ozarks began to fade. Through Lebanon, where Route 66 nostalgia meets modern truck stop culture, then Springfield, where the Ozark hills make their last stand before surrendering to the prairie.

"Watch how the land changes," Gus's voice came through the intercom. "You can feel the continent opening up."

As they crossed into Kansas, the transformation became complete. The horizon suddenly extended forever, and the old bikes leaned into a constant prairie wind. Through Fort Scott, where Civil War history lived in restored brick buildings, then Iola, where the town square felt like a scene from another era.

"These airheads love this kind of riding," Gus said during

a fuel stop in Yates Center. "They were built for distance." The bikes drew attention from locals, their classic lines a contrast to modern machines.

The towns became more sparse, the distances between them grew. Eureka, with its cattle auction yards that were still active. El Dorado, where oil derricks dotted the horizon. The wind grew stronger, teaching Sam about the art of the constant lean.

They rode through Wichita's sprawl, then out again into pure prairie. The small towns seemed to exist mainly to service the vast wheat fields—Garden Plain, Kingman, Pratt. Each one a self-contained world with its grain elevators standing like cathedrals against the endless sky.

"Different kind of navigation out here," Gus noted as they rested in Greensburg, a town rebuilt after a devastating tornado. "You navigate by elevator towers instead of mountains."

Somewhere in Kansas, the world went flat. The highway stretched ahead like a ruler line drawn to the horizon, and the sky opened up into something so vast it made Sam's chest tight. The pair had left the last town twenty miles back and Sam felt like he was sailing across the Atlantic Ocean in a little boat. He thought about the part in *Don Quixote* where the old man was gathering his weapons, preparing for his first adventure.

And the first thing he did was to polish up his armor, which had belonged to his great-grandfather and had lain forgotten in a corner, covered with rust and mold. He cleaned it and repaired it as best he could, but he noticed one great defect: it had no helmet, only a simple headpiece. His ingenuity supplied this deficiency, for he made a kind of half-helmet out of pasteboard, which, when attached to the headpiece, gave the appearance of a complete helmet. True, when he came to test its strength by drawing his sword and giving it a couple of slashes, the first one destroyed in an instant what had taken him a week to create. This ease with which it was destroyed troubled him, and to guard against a similar misfortune, he made another one, reinforcing it with strips of iron.

The narrator's voice in Sam's helmet competed with the steady thrum of the motorcycle and the wind that found every gap in his jacket. Gus's bike cut through the morning air like a compass needle pointing west. Fields of wheat rippled on either side of them, like golden waves that stretched to the horizon. The sun was still low enough to cast long shadows, but Sam could feel its growing strength on his back.

In a village of La Mancha, the name of which I have no desire to recall...

The opening line had hit differently at sixty-five miles per hour than it had when Sam had first glanced at the paperback copy Dr. Fitz had given him. There was something about being in motion, about watching the landscape unfold, that made the words feel immediate and alive. Don Quixote was leaving everything he knew, convinced he understood something everyone else had missed. Sam thought about the way Don Quixote gathered his grandfather's old armor, how he'd cleaned and repaired it as best he could.

Just the day before, Sam had watched his granddad doing essentially the same thing, methodically checking the bikes in the pre-dawn darkness of the campground. He checked tire pressure, throttle and clutch cable play, and oil level, his hands moving over the metal with practiced care, a ritual repeated so many times it had become something like prayer.

Having thus cleaned his armor and made a full helmet out of a simple headpiece, and having given a name to his horse and fixed upon one for himself, he decided that nothing more was needed except to look for a lady to be in love with...

A truck passed them going east, its wake buffeting the bikes. Sam adjusted his grip and relaxed his shoulders, remembering Gus's lessons about letting the bike find its own balance. Ahead of them, a cluster of wind turbines rose from the wheat fields, their massive blades turning with dreamlike slowness against the blue sky. The sight triggered something in his mind—hadn't Don Quixote fought windmills? Thought they were giants?

Sam squinted at the turbines through his visor. They did look like giants, in a way. Their shadows swept across the wheat like reaching arms, and their size became more imposing the closer they got. Sam wondered what Don Quixote would make of them—these actual giants built and planted in the fields.

The narrator was describing Sancho Panza, the practical farmer who somehow got caught up in Don Quixote's grand delusion. Sam thought about the way Gus had described Phil the night before. "Imagine meeting Don Quixote in real life," he'd said. If Phil was Don Quixote, did that make Gus Sancho Panza? The loyal friend who followed even when he knew better?

Grandfather and grandson passed another mile marker, its number meaningless in the endless landscape. The wheat fields had finally given way to pastureland, where black cattle stood like ink drops on green paper. In Sam's helmet, Don Quixote was explaining his vision of knight-errantry to a bewildered Sancho, laying out all the wrongs they would right, all the injustices they would correct.

A knight errant, Sancho, is one who rights wrongs, protects the innocent, and seeks justice even when others see only folly. For it is not enough to see the world as it is—one must see it as it ought to be, and work to make it so.

Gus and Sam stopped at a rest area in Mill Creek, Kansas, not far from where the Keystone pipeline ruptured in December 2022. The prairie stretched out before them, deceptively peaceful under the summer sun.

"Almost 600,000 gallons of crude oil," Gus said, looking toward the creek that gave the town its name. "Biggest onshore crude oil spill in the United States in nearly a decade. Spread through Mill Creek, contaminated the soil, killed wildlife."

Sam shielded his eyes against the sun. "Can you still see it?"

"That's the thing about oil spills—they leave marks that

last generations. The visible cleanup might be done, but the chemicals persist in the soil, in the groundwater." Gus took off his riding gloves. "TC Energy, the company that owned the pipeline, said all the right things. Promised to make it right, take responsibility." He then uttered to himself, "Same words we heard from Peterson Energy forty years ago."

A freight train rumbled past in the distance, carrying oil tankers west.

"You know what bothers me most?" Gus continued. "The pipeline was supposedly state-of-the-art. Had all the latest safety features. But it still failed. Just like they all eventually do. And each time, the companies act surprised, like they couldn't have seen it coming."

"Even though their own engineers probably warned them?"

"You're right about that. There's almost always someone inside who knows the risks, writes the memos, tries to prevent the disaster." Gus zipped up his jacket against the prairie wind. "But profit wins out over prudence every time."

They mounted their bikes, ready to continue west, while behind them Mill Creek flowed on, carrying invisible memories of what corporate negligence looks like when it spills across the prairie.

Sam remembered what Dr. Fitz had said about sometimes needing to read other people's stories before you could understand your own. Out here, with nothing but road and sky and story, Sam was beginning to see what he meant. Every mile took them further from the life Sam thought he was supposed to live, closer to... what? A story about an old prosecutor who tilted at windmills disguised as energy companies?

The sun got higher and heat waves shimmered on the highway ahead, making it look like the road was floating. In Sam's ears, Don Quixote and Sancho were setting out on their adventure, leaving behind the world of common sense for something larger and more dangerous. Something that everyone else thought was madness.

Sam watched the fields go past them as the old motorcycles carried them unwavering in their westward course. The wind turbines were behind them, their shadows no longer visible. But when Sam checked his mirror, they still looked like giants on the horizon, their arms slowly turning against the morning sky.

In short, our gentleman became so caught up in reading that he spent his nights from sunset to sunrise and his days from dawn to dark poring over his books, and from so little sleeping and so much reading, his brain dried up and he lost his sanity...

Sam had smiled inside his helmet when he first heard this. Maybe that's what this whole journey was—a shared madness, a story they were choosing to believe in. And maybe that wasn't such a bad thing.

An hour later the Kansas wind hit them like a living thing. Through Sam's helmet speakers, Don Quixote's words seem perfectly suited to the moment: *Observe, friend Sancho, how capricious the winds that beset us, howling like all the devils of hell let loose. Yet a true knight must lean into such adversity, for nature's fury tests the mettle of both steed and rider.*

There were no trees, no hills, nothing to break the wind's force as it swept across the prairie. Sam's motorcycle leaned into it at a constant angle, the old airhead engine steady despite the buffeting. His left side felt stretched, his right compressed, holding the bike in its perpetual lean against the crosswind.

"Fifteen degrees off center," Gus's voice came through the intercom. "Like sailing into a quartering wind. Let the bike find its angle."

The wind picked up even more and Sam clenched his handlebars in fright as he watched tumbleweeds race across the highway ahead of them. Wind turbines on the horizon turn lazily, while closer at hand, the wheat fields rippled like ocean waves. The bikes required constant attention—a gust could push them halfway into the other lane if they were not ready for it

Another passage from the book floated through Sam's mind: *When the tempest rages, that is when a knight must show his calmness, letting his resolve stand firm as a windmill against the gale.* Sam almost laughed at the windmill reference, thinking about how different these modern structures were from Don Quixote's imagined foes.

Road signs vibrated wildly on their posts. When they passed the occasional truck, there was a moment of calm in its wind shadow, then the wall of prairie wind slammed back into them. The BMW's windshield helped, but Sam felt every muscle working to maintain their course.

"Watch for the wind shadows behind buildings and trees," Gus warned. "The sudden lack of pressure can be as tricky as the wind itself."

They were making their own weather at sixty miles per hour—the wind in their faces well over eighty. The old bike felt like a ship tacking against a gale, its boxer engine throbbing steadily below, unnaturally calm against the chaos around them. Sam began to understand why they call it the Great Plains—there's nothing small about the empty vastness where wind ruled supreme.

Another grain elevator appeared ahead, massive against the sky. "Brace yourself," Gus called. "Wind'll drop to nothing in its shadow, then hit us double when we clear it."

Sam felt it happen—the sudden eerie calm, his arms automatically adjusting as the bike straightened, then the violent punch of the wind returning. But beneath him, the old bike simply adjusted and carried on, as steady as ever, like Don Quixote's Rocinante facing his own windswept adventures, teaching Sam something about persistence in the face of natural forces.

The wind finally calmed down and then almost stopped. Soon afterwards Gus's left hand dropped, signaling a gas stop ahead. Sam nodded, though his grandfather couldn't see him, and began watching for the exit. In his helmet, Don Quixote rode on, chasing windmills and glory, while his story wound itself through the landscape like a thread through some sort of tapestry, connecting everything Sam was seeing to everything he was hearing.

Without the wind, heat ripples rose from the prairie as Gus led them into the Boot Hill Campground. The sun sat low on the horizon, turning the grass to copper. They chose a nice spot sheltered by a stand of cottonwoods, where the leaves rustled in the evening breeze.

Sam had quickly figured out the routine: bikes on their center stands, facing east for morning sun. With each passing day they unpacked with practiced efficiency—tents, sleeping bags, camp stove. Sam noticed how his grandfather placed everything just so, a habit, he said, from decades of setting up courtroom exhibits.

"Weather's building," Gus said, nodding toward thunderheads stacking up in the distance. They made sure to secure the rain flies, even though the storm looked hours away.

"Yeah, I don't care for those thunderstorms," Sam replied. "Do they make you nervous?"

"Lots of things make me nervous, especially when I'm on a motorcycle. That includes thunderstorms, rain, and especially a strong cross wind." Gus thought for a moment and then added, "Add animals on the road and all those drivers on their phones."

"So why do you like riding these motorcycles so much if they make you anxious?"

"I guess my best answer goes back to when we were talking about being anxious at school. For me, the way to deal with your fears is to face them directly and not try to avoid them. What I like about riding these old bikes is that it makes me pay attention. I mean really pay attention. As you know by now, if you stop paying attention and start getting sloppy then you will be in trouble, fast. Riding a motorcycle forces you to focus and to be aware of everything going on around you. And, of course, the more you practice the better you get." He paused for a second. "Hmm. Maybe not a bad way to approach your life, eh?"

The sun dropped behind Dodge City's grain elevators while they heated soup on the camp stove. Heat lightning flickered on the horizon, nature's own testimony about what was coming. In Sam's helmet, still warm from the day's ride, Don Quixote waited to continue his journey toward truth and justice.

Gus spread their map on the picnic table, weighing down the corners with stones. "Long day tomorrow," he said, tracing their route with his finger. "We'll hit Boulder by sunset if we start early. Camp in the foothills." His finger moved south. "Then down through Colorado into New Mexico. That's where the real story begins."

"How long to Santa Fe?" Sam asked.

"Two days from Boulder, if we take our time. We stop at Ghost Ranch first. You need to see those red cliffs to understand what Phil saw. Why he chose to fight the battles he did."

Above them, the first stars appeared while distant thunder muttered promises of rain.

CHAPTER 13

KANSAS TO COLORADO

They rode past Dodge City as dawn broke across the prairie, their headlights cutting through lingering darkness. The morning air carried the scent of cattle and wheat, while ahead, Highway 50 stretched toward a horizon that seemed impossibly distant.

They rode through Garden City, where massive feedlots announced themselves to their noses before their eyes. Then Holcomb, infamous from Truman Capote's *In Cold Blood*, now just another quiet Kansas town. The bikes maintained their steady rhythm against the constant prairie wind, which required a perpetual lean to hold their line.

"Mountains are out there," Gus's voice crackled through the intercom. "Even though we can't see them yet."

Syracuse, Coolidge, and finally the Colorado border. The transformation was subtle at first—a slightly higher elevation, the grass growing shorter, the air was becoming noticeably thinner.

Through Las Animas and La Junta, where the Arkansas River valley provided some unexpected green in the brown landscape. Then Pueblo, where finally, impossibly, the Rockies appeared on the horizon—at first they looked like clouds, then with each mile they resolved into mountains that seem unreal in their scale that dominated the western sky completely.

They stopped in Colorado Springs for Gus to adjust the carburetors again because of the altitude and thin air. The bikes drew attention at the gas station—their classic lines a contrast to the modern SUVs and mountain bikes along the way.

"Different world from Kansas," Gus observed.

"Yes! These mountains are just unbelievable!" Sam responded.

"Like walking into a cathedral," Gus said. "No matter how many times I've see them, they still take my breath away."

After a few minutes Gus spoke again. "It's another ninety miles north to get to Boulder. It's sort of a detour and I just wanted to double check that you're alright doing the extra miles, instead of going due west from here and then south to New Mexico."

"Fine with me," Sam said. "I remember you pointed that out when we were planning the route."

As they rode the air got cooler, crisper with each mile north along the Front Range. Through Castle Rock,

Littleton, and Denver's sprawling suburbs.

They stopped at a viewpoint outside Denver, where the Front Range mountains provided a dramatic backdrop to the city sprawl. Gus pointed toward a series of ponds near a power plant, their surfaces deceptively calm in the afternoon light.

"See those?" he said. "Coal ash impoundments. The dirty secret of 'clean coal'—what's left after they burn it has to go somewhere."

Sam gazed at the innocuous-looking ponds. "Doesn't seem that dangerous."

"That's the problem. It never does." Gus leaned against his bike. "Back in 2008, just east of here in Weld County, one of those impoundments failed. Spilled thousands of tons of coal ash into the South Platte River watershed. Heavy metals, arsenic, selenium, mercury—all the toxic byproducts of coal burning suddenly in the water supply."

A hawk circled overhead, riding the thermals from the city below.

"The company knew the containment was failing," Gus continued. "Their own engineers had flagged it years earlier. But fixing it properly would have cost money, cut into profits. So they did the minimum, hoped for the best."

"Like Phil's case with the energy company?"

"Same pattern. Corporate knowledge, deliberate inaction, devastating consequences." Gus watched a train carrying coal rumble along the valley floor. "The really insidious part? Coal ash isn't classified as hazardous waste under federal regulations, even though it contains compounds that would be strictly regulated in any other industry."

"How'd they manage that?"

"Lobbying. Political donations. The usual tools big corporations use to shape the rules in their favor." He turned back to Sam. "After the spill, did the company executives go to jail? No. Did they even pay the full cleanup costs? No. Most of that fell to taxpayers, while the profits stayed private."

"So what happened to the people affected? The communities?"

"Some are still fighting in court, fifteen years later. Others gave up, moved away if they could afford to. The poor ones?" Gus shook his head. "They keep drinking the water, growing gardens in contaminated soil, watching cancer rates climb while the company issues statements about 'no proven causation.'"

The city spread below them, its buildings gleamed in the afternoon sun, while invisible in the groundwater, the legacy of corporate decisions continued its slow migration through the ecosystem.

The final stretch to Boulder took them through a landscape that couldn't be more different from where they started that morning. The plains ended abruptly at the Flatirons, the distinctive slabs of stone that guard Boulder's western edge. The old bikes climbed the last few miles easily, their engines happy in the cooling air.

They arrived in Boulder as the afternoon light turned

the Flatirons to gold. Behind them lay a day's worth of trans-formation—from endless prairie to soaring peaks, from cattle towns to a university city, from one version of the American West to another.

They camped in Boulder, at a site tucked against the foothills. The mountains loomed above them, catching the last light while the valley fell into shadow. The campground sat in a grove of ponderosa pines, their bark smelled almost of vanilla in the evening warmth. The famed Flatirons rose above them like the bows of ancient ships, catching the last sunlight. Sam was dumbfounded as he watched climbers descend from their routes, looking like slow tiny spiders against the stone.

"I wonder what it's like to be climbing one of those cliffs?" Sam asked.

Gus looked up to see what he was talking about. "I guess the climbers are roped in, but to be honest, I can't imagine anything worse! I'm not a big fan of heights."

"Really? I thought you probably did that kind of thing when you were younger."

Gus laughed. "Oh no, I did a lot of wild stuff, often under the influence of something or other, just like you guys probably do, but I inherited a healthy fear of heights from my father. So, it was no cliff climbing for me." He paused, and then added, "Although, I guess if someone dared me to do it, I probably would have."

Sam nodded. "Yeah, I know that feeling."

"One of the few good things about getting older is that

you feel less pressure to do those things way outside your comfort zone. Although, of course, some pressure never hurts. It's what keeps us sharp." He thought for a second and added, "I must say, the thought of getting humiliated, either real or imagined, is still a big motivator for me to step up to the challenge."

"I hadn't thought about it, but I guess that is something pretty cool about that Don Quixote character," Sam responded lightheartedly. "I mean he wasn't swayed by what anyone around him thought about him. I mean everyone thought he was nuts and he just kept on doing his thing."

"You're right, he was pretty fearless."

"Fearless." Sam nodded as he poked at the fire with a stick, gathering his thoughts.

"Everyone keeps talking about college like it's the only path worth taking," he finally said. "My parents, the counselors, Ellen—they all act like anything else is failure."

Gus waited, letting the silence give Sam space to continue.

"But I look at their lives—all these successful people with their degrees. Dad in his corporate law firm, mom with her MBA, my teachers with their certifications. They're all just... stuck. Following rules, filling out forms, measuring success in quarterly reports."

The fire crackled, sending sparks toward into the sky.

"I watch them, you know? How they talk about their jobs like they're serving time. How they live for weekends and vacations. How they keep buying things to make up for the lives they're not living." He looked at Gus. "Even my teachers—they teach the same books the same way every year, never asking why anymore, just following the curriculum." Pausing, he added, "Well, I guess I would not include Dr. Fitz in that particular generalization."

"And you want something different?"

"I want something real. Something that matters." Sam gestured at their bikes, at the road ahead. "When you work on those old BMWs, you know exactly why you're doing each thing. When you defended someone in court, you were fighting for something concrete. But college..." He shook his head. "It feels like a delay tactic. Four more years of sitting in rooms while the real world happens somewhere else."

"Your father would say you're being impractical."

"Maybe. But watching him chase billable hours, watching mom stress about corporate budgets—that doesn't seem practical either. It seems like a trap. Like they're all running on this hamster wheel of degrees and promotions and mortgages, too tired to ask if it's what they really want."

The night deepened around them while Sam added another log to the fire.

"I don't know what I want to do yet," he admitted. "But I know I want it to matter. To make some kind of difference. Not just... follow a script someone else wrote."

Gus nodded slowly. "Sounds like someone else I knew. A prosecutor who decided to fight giants when everyone else was chasing windmills."

They ate their pasta dinner watching a mule deer graze

at the edge of their camp, the animal unbothered by human presence. Boulder's lights began to twinkle below them while above, the mountains turned purple with the evening.

"Ghost Ranch tomorrow," Gus said as he pulled out the map. "Georgia O'Keeffe country. Red cliffs, blue sky, the kind of place that makes you understand why people paint pictures or tell stories." His finger moved to Santa Fe. "Then here, where the real story begins."

"Phil's story?"

"Actually, he had a team, so you could say it is our story. All of us who saw something that needed telling." Gus folded the map. "The landscape down there... it has a way of making truth visible. You'll see."

Above them, stars lit the sky in ancient patterns, while somewhere ahead, the road waited with its own lessons about choosing paths and finding purpose.

CHAPTER 14

COLORADO TO NEW MEXICO

Morning brought frost on their tents. They packed quickly, eager to warm up through movement. The descent from the Front Range took them through canyons where the morning sun hadn't reached, and Sam was near frozen, his breath visible in his helmet.

The western slope of the Rockies revealed itself in layers—high peaks giving way to mesas, mesas falling into canyons. They stopped at a pullout where a sign marked the Continental Divide, while the bikes' engines made a ticking sound as they cooled.

They rode through Nederland, where Gus told Sam that old hippies and new tech workers shared coffee shops, and then went south along the Peak to Peak Highway. "Watch for elk," Gus's voice came through the intercom. "They like these mountain meadows at dawn."

The pair then dropped down to Central City, its casino lights still blinking in the morning sun, then through Black Hawk, where Colorado's mining history met modern gambling. The road demanded lots of attention—switchbacks and dramatic elevation changes that tested both riders and their machines.

Through Idaho Springs, Georgetown, and Silverplume—old mining towns strung like beads along the highway. Then they headed south toward Fairplay, where South Park opened up around them, a high-altitude prairie ringed by peaks.

"Air's getting thin up here," Gus noted during a stop to adjust the carburetors again. "Bikes are telling us they need more fuel."

They descended through Salida, where the Arkansas River drew kayakers and rafters, then into the San Luis Valley—a vast high desert bowl that marked the beginning of New Mexico's influence. Alamosa appeared like a mirage, its adobe buildings and Hispanic culture previewing what lay ahead.

As the two crossed into New Mexico, the landscape transformed. They rode through Taos, where ancient pueblo met artist colony, and the architecture changed from mountain rustic to adobe.

"What's that smell in the air?" Sam asked.

"The air carries the scent of sage and piñon pine," Gus told him. "And if you ask me, the quality of the light has shifted as well. Down here it is clearer, more intense."

"Different kind of mountains here," Gus observed an hour later as they passed through Española. "These were born in fire, not collision."

The final stretch to Ghost Ranch took them through Rio Arriba County and into Abiquiu, Georgia O'Keeffe country, where red rocks and blue sky created the palette she made famous.

• • • • •

"Everything changes from here," Gus said to Sam. "Watch how the landscape transforms."

The 21,000 acre retreat and education center called Ghost Ranch emerged like something from a painting—which, Sam realized, it was. The same red and orange cliffs he'd seen in art museums rose around them, their layers telling stories older than humanity. The road to Ghost Ranch took them through layers of red and orange stone, each formation more dramatic than the last.

The pair parked their bikes near the visitor center, and Gus led Sam to a viewpoint overlooking Chimney Rock. "Georgia O'Keeffe first came here in 1934," he said, gesturing at the vast landscape. "She was already famous for her New York paintings, but something about this place called to her. Said she knew it was her country as soon as she saw it."

The late afternoon light transformed the cliffs into the same colors Sam remembered from O'Keeffe's paintings in the art books he had browsed.

"She'd spend hours just looking at these rocks," Gus continued. "People thought she was eccentric, sitting out here alone, staring at cliffs. But she saw something others missed. The way light changes stone, how shadows hold color, how the landscape tells stories if you learn to read it."

A half hour later they rode the short distance to Abiquiu, the ancient pueblo village where O'Keeffe made her home. The adobe buildings seemed to grow from the earth itself, their walls the same color as the surrounding cliffs.

"This whole area is sacred to the Tewa people," Gus explained as they paused near the plaza. "They've lived here for over a thousand years. Called it 'the place of singing waters' because of the streams that once ran more freely through these canyons." He pointed to the mesa rising behind the village. "That's Tsi-pin, their ancestral home. Every rock, every spring, every cliff has a story, a spiritual significance."

An elderly woman selling pottery nodded at Gus's words. "The old ones knew how to listen to the land," she said. "They understood that everything here is connected—the water, the clay, the light itself."

A bit later the two found a place to stop for the night with a view of the Pedernal, the flat-topped mountain O'Keeffe often painted. They made camp beneath a grove of cottonwood trees, their leaves shimmering silver in the late afternoon breeze.

"O'Keeffe painted these cliffs for decades," Gus said as

they set up their tents. "Said she had to keep painting them because no one would believe they really looked like this."

"She used to say God told her if she painted that mountain enough times, she could have it," Gus said. "When she died, they scattered her ashes there. But the Tewa people knew the mountain's power long before O'Keeffe arrived. They call it Tsi-mayoh, the 'rock on high.' It's featured in their creation stories."

"How do you know all this stuff?" Sam wanted to know.

"We lived here for years and I fell in love with this land, the people, the history, the art, everything." Gus responded with a smile. "And, of course, they don't call New Mexico the 'Land of Enchantment' for nothing.

The sunset soon turned the rocks to a bright orange color while they heated their dinner on their camp stove. Sam thought about how O'Keeffe saw beauty where others saw empty desert, about how his grandfather said his boss saw fraud where others saw only business as usual, and about how the Tewa people saw sacred connections where others saw resources to be exploited.

"You know what Phil would have loved about this place?" Gus asked, pouring coffee. "How many different ways there are of seeing truth here. O'Keeffe with her artist's eye, the Tewa people with their spiritual understanding, even the Spanish settlers who built these churches and called the land holy."

"The Tewa have a saying," Gus added as they started to put out the fire for the night. "'The land is alive.' They don't just mean the plants and animals. They mean everything—the rocks, the sky, the light itself. Makes you think about what Phil was fighting for, doesn't it? Not just against pollution and climate change, but for a different way of seeing our relationship with the earth."

Just then Sam remembered a passage from his audiobook he wanted to share. "Listen to how Don Quixote explains being a knight," he said after a moment.

Know, Sancho, that the first law of knighthood is to protect the weak, defend the helpless, and pursue justice wherever it may lead. A knight must face all perils with steadfast heart, serve his lady with unwavering devotion, and keep his honor bright as his sword. For chivalry demands not only courage in battle, but nobility in thought and deed. We must protect those who cannot protect themselves, speak truth to power, and maintain our virtue even when all mock our quest.

"Is that what was going on with you and Phil?" Sam asked.

"Yeah, I'd say that's what drew me to Phil's case at first," Gus said, adding a small piece of wood to their fire. "Not just the legal challenge, but the idea that someone had to stand up for those who couldn't fight for themselves. The communities affected by pollution, the future generations who would inherit what we left them."

"But what about the lady part?" Sam asks. "Phil wasn't fighting for a specific woman."

"No, but you might say he was fighting for Mother Earth herself," Gus replied.

Sam felt the night envelope him and his grandfather. It was filled with a kind of silence that felt like some sort of wisdom. Sam heard a coyote call from somewhere in the darkness with its voice echoing off the cliffs around them. Above them, the stars emerged over the red cliffs while they considered how ancient ideals of knighthood might translate into modern battles for justice.

CHAPTER 15

NEW MEXICO

After a mid-morning start, Sam and Gus headed south. The New Mexico landscape spread out in colors Sam didn't really have names for—rust and copper and something between purple and brown. The Sangre de Cristo Mountains rose in the distance like big ocean waves that were frozen in stone, their shadows stretched across plains that were dotted with sage and yucca.

Gus led them off the main highway onto a smaller road that wound through red rock formations. The afternoon sun turned everything to fire—the cliffs, the sand, even the air itself seemed to burn. The two stopped at an overlook where a wooden cross stood against the sky, weathered to a silvery color by the sun and wind.

"This is where it started," Gus said, killing his engine. "Where Phil first told me about his idea."

Sam pulled off his helmet, sweat immediately

evaporating in the dry air. Below them, the valley stretched for miles, broken by rocky outcrops against the vast landscape. "What idea?"

Gus walked to the edge of the overlook, his boots crunching on gravel. He pointed to the east, past the horizon. "You can't see it, but there was a cluster of industrial buildings about a hundred miles that way, over in Mora County. That was the Peterson Energy complex. It used to be one of the biggest coal-fired power plants in the Southwest."

"Used to be?"

"They shut it down in 2010. But back in '86, it was running full blast. Sending up smoke signals you could see from space." He turned to face Sam. "Phil brought me over there my first week on the job. Said he wanted to show me what we were really fighting."

Sam felt the wind pick up, hot and dry, carrying the scent of sage. A raven called somewhere below, its cry echoed off the rocks. "Fighting how?"

"Phil had this crazy idea." Gus smiled, but it didn't reach his eyes. "He wanted to charge them with murder."

• • • • •

The two rode on to Santa Fe and parked at the Plaza, which was in the center of town. After walking around the central plaza and visiting a few of the dozens of art galleries, they stopped to eat enchiladas covered in red and green chili at a restaurant call The Shed. Afterwards, they rode to the Hyde Recreation Area outside of town and set up camp. That evening, they sat by the fire. Sam thought about the latest chapters in his audiobook and Don Quixote's absolute certainty about his missions. About how everyone else saw madness, but he saw purpose.

He thought about what Gus told him at the overlook. About how his boss, Phil Stone, looked out toward that power plant and saw something no one else saw. Or maybe something everyone saw but no one dared to name.

In Sam's head, the stories were starting to overlap—Don Quixote with his windmills, his grandfather talking about Phil with his power plants. Both of them tilting at giants that everyone else called progress, or necessity, or just the way things were. And, of course, maybe the whole lot of them were crazy, he thought.

Sam could not help but think about Gus when the narrator described how Sancho Panza followed Don Quixote despite knowing his master was mad. But was it really madness to see the truth and refuse to look away? Was it crazy to fight battles that everyone else said couldn't be won?

Beyond the tents, the desert night was alive with small sounds—wind through juniper trees, distant coyotes. Sam remembered that Dr. Fitz talked about stories starting with the wrong choice for the right reasons. About how sometimes the crazy choice and the right choice looked exactly the same.

"Phil used to say that everything looks different in the

desert," Gus remarked after taking a sip of coffee. "Said it was because there's nowhere to hide out there. Everything's exposed."

"So what happened?" Sam asked. "With the case?"

"Keep listening to your Don Quixote," he said. "The part about what happens when he actually reaches those things he sees as unjust or evil."

"You know that's not an answer."

"No?" He chuckled. "Then maybe you're not far enough into the story yet."

"Granddad?"

"Mm?"

"Are you telling me that Phil really thought he could win? Charging the power companies with murder?"

"Ah." Sam could hear something changed in his voice. "That's the interesting thing about Don Quixote, isn't it? Everyone remembers that he fought windmills. They forget to ask if maybe, just maybe, he was right about them all along."

CHAPTER 16

SANTA FE

The next morning over a breakfast of pastry rolls and coffee, Gus told Sam the story of how he first met Phil.

"I was at the state's Attorney General's office in Santa Fe. I'd been there maybe two or three days. I expected the usual—handshakes, small talk, maybe some gentle warnings about managing my expectations. Phil was standing on his desk trying to hang a map of New Mexico and he told me to help him. The map was marked with red dots and lines I couldn't quite make sense of.

"He jumped down from the desk. "What do you know about cancer clusters?" was the first thing he asked me. I didn't know so he told me that cancer clusters were statistical anomalies in cancer rates within specific geographic areas. And then he started pointing at the red dots on the map and said that each one represented a death. Each one had a name, a family, a story."

Sam thought this was a strange recitation but was still paying attention. "So, what was that all about?"

Gus continued. "I told him that I thought this was the criminal division, not the civil division." He looked at Sam. "So you know, a civil law suit is about money whereas a criminal case is about punishing the defendant with things like jail and other penalties.

"He told me it was. He asked me if I knew the difference between knowing someone is dying because of your actions and pulling a trigger? So, I gave him a pretty good answer. I said 'Legally? Several hundred years of precedent.' Phil smiled at me and told me it was a good answer. Wrong, but good."

Sam sat up and looked over at his grandfather. Shaking his head, he tried to figure out if the old man was just telling him some story he had concocted to glorify his younger days in New Mexico. He furrowed his eyebrows to signal his skepticism. "Okay. So then what happened."

Gus took a sip of coffee. He smiled at Sam and looked into the fire as he continued. "I'll tell you this, Sam. Phil's office looked like a war room by my third week. The map of New Mexico was covered in overlapping circles of red string, connecting death certificates to weather patterns to power plant locations. Stacks of medical journals and environmental reports covered every surface, and one entire wall was dedicated to what Phil called "the knowledge time-line"—internal memos and research reports from energy companies dating back to the 1950s.

"Phil then pulled out an old document protected in a plastic sleeve. I remember it clearly. "In 1957," he told me, "their own scientists warned about carbon dioxide buildup in the atmosphere. Predicting temperature increases, weather pattern changes, respiratory diseases."

Gus shook his head and stood up from the campfire, stretched for a minute and then poured himself more coffee.

"So, what happened after that?" Sam asked.

Gus stared into the fire. "They knew," he said. "Phil showed me another document. It was a 1968 internal memo about increased mortality rates in communities downwind of coal plants. Then another, in 1972—a study linking particulate matter to childhood asthma cases. And another in 1975—projected cancer rates in exposure zones. Phil was so pissed off. I remember he spun around and almost shouted in my face. 'They knew,' Phil shouted. 'They documented it, and they buried it.'"

Sam nodded. "This is getting interesting. So, what next?"

Gus continued. " 'Knowledge isn't the same as causation,' I told him. Then, thinking of my corporate law classes at law school, I reminded him that you'd need to prove specific intent.

"Phil was ready for that and asked me 'What do you call it when you know your actions will result in death, but you do them anyway?' He pulled out another file and told me in no uncertain terms, 'In criminal law, we call that depraved indifference to human life. It's a foundation for homicide charges.'

"So, I thought about what he said and started to tell him, 'No prosecutor has ever...'"

Gus looked over at Sam. "Before I could even finish my sentence, he said, 'Because no prosecutor has had this.' And then he spread another set of documents across the desk. He was really pumped up and told me that three weeks prior, a whistleblower from Peterson Energy contacted him with internal communications showing they actively suppressed these studies. They had redirected research funds and even launched disinformation campaigns."

Gus kept on. "I remember picking up one of the memos. All I could think to say was that they would bury us in motions. Jurisdictional challenges, statute of limitations..."

Gus pointed his finger at the fire as if to reenact the scene, " 'Read page four,' Phil told me. So I flipped through the document and halfway down the page, a paragraph jumped out. It said something like 'Continued operation of the southwestern facilities will result in an estimated 4,000 excess deaths over the next decade.' And then there was a recommendation to maintain current opacity levels in public disclosures."

"Really?" Sam shook his head. "It really said that?"

Gus nodded, "Yup, and that's not all. Phil pulled out another document, telling me that they tracked the deaths. Mapped them. They created actuarial tables to calculate the cost-benefit ratio of human lives against profit margins."

Gus paused to let this sink in.

"So, what happened after all that?" Sam asked.

"I told Phil that I didn't think the law was designed for that kind of case, a criminal case. I remember his eyes were burning and he slammed his fist on the desk and almost shouted that the law was designed for exactly this kind of case. He said that when someone knows their actions will cause death, takes steps to hide that knowledge, and does it anyway—that was not negligence. That was not civil liability. That was homicide!"

Gus stopped for a moment to gather himself, and then looked at Sam. "I remember that he walked to the map, tracing one of the red strings. He said, 'Maria Valdez, age nine. Acute respiratory failure after three years of chronic bronchial inflammation. Lived her whole life in the fallout zone of the Peterson plant.' His finger moved to another point. 'James Running Horse, age sixty-two. Lung cancer. No history of smoking. Twenty years downwind of the same facility.'

"I figured that I was there mostly as a sounding board for Phil. I had learned that he had a somewhat questionable reputation for going after businesses and corporations for committing fraud by their misrepresenting things. I told him they would say we couldn't prove individual causation."

"What's that mean?" Sam asked.

"It means that it would be hard to pin a particular death to a particular person or particular act," Gus explained. He then added, "That's a good question and that's what I was pointing out to Phil. That it would be hard to make a direct connection, especially in a criminal case charging murder or homicide, where you have to prove all the elements of the charge by proof beyond a reasonable doubt, which is a very high burden."

Sam was getting confused with the legal jargon his grandfather was using, but pretty much understood the gist and nodded to encourage him to continue.

Gus could see Sam losing his focus on what he was saying, so he quickly moved on with the story. "But Phil said that we could prove they knew there would be deaths. We could prove they calculated the number of deaths. We could prove they hid this knowledge and kept operating anyway. I remember he turned to me and illustrated by asking, 'If I hand you a bomb and tell you it will kill people if you throw it, and you throw it anyway, that's murder.' And how was this different?"

This made sense to Sam, but he still couldn't quite tell if this investigation, this case, all really happened or if his grandfather was making some, or all, of it up. "So, then what?"

"So, I looked at the map again, saw it with new eyes, where each red dot was a person. Each string connected a death to a decision made in a boardroom by people who thought the law couldn't touch them. I remember telling Phil that they will say he was crazy. Tilting at windmills."

Sam perked up. "You didn't really say that, did you?"

Gus nodded his head and smiled. "He asked me if I

knew what everyone forgets about Don Quixote. And then he gathered up the documents and answered the question himself. 'He didn't fight the windmills because he was crazy. He fought them because everyone else was too sane to see what they really were."

Sam sat back. He had enjoyed seeing his grandfather get excited and the enthusiasm with which he had told the story. "So, Granddad, is there an ending to this story? Are you going to tell me what happened after all this?"

Gus paused for a second and then added, "I'll tell you that in my briefcase, back then, the files felt heavy with more than just paper. They felt heavy with truth, with purpose, with the weight of all those red dots on Phil's map. That night, I started reading and by dawn I knew I was all in."

CHAPTER 17

THE EVIDENCE

The late morning sun gilded Santa Fe's adobe buildings as Gus led Sam on a walking tour around the Plaza. The air carried the scent of piñon smoke and Sam could smell the fresh-baked bread from the cafes opening for breakfast.

"The Palace of the Governors," Gus said, gesturing to the long, low building on the Plaza's north side. "Oldest public building in America. Spanish built it in 1610. Now it's Navajo and Pueblo artists selling jewelry under the portal."

They walked east, past the cathedral, toward the state government complex. The New Mexico State Capitol stood distinctive among the adobe architecture—still southwestern in style but was larger, more imposing.

"The Roundhouse, they call it," Gus explained. "Only

round state capitol in the country. Inside, there's a collection of New Mexican art that tells the state's story better than any history book. That's also where the Attorney General's Office is located."

"Is that where your office was?" Sam asked.

"Yes, we were up on the second floor. It was nice. We prosecuted cases all over the state but that's where our main office was located. We also had a satellite office down in Albuquerque."

"That's a really cool looking place," Sam nodded with a grin.

It was when they reached the judicial complex that Gus's pace slowed and his voice took on a different tone. "This is where Phil fought many of his battles," he said, stopping before the courthouse. "Where we presented evidence to the grand jury and tried cases. Where we believed we could make power answer to truth."

Sam looked up at the building. "Where you brought the case against Peterson Energy?"

"Right here." Gus pointed to the steps. "That's where Phil announced the indictments. Press everywhere. Company lawyers looking like they'd swallowed something sour." He smiled at the memory. "For one brief moment, they had to answer for what they'd done."

They walked around to the back of the building, where a small garden grew in a protected courtyard. "Phil's victory garden," Gus says softly. "Every time they tore it up, he'd plant more. Some of these plants are probably descendants of his original ones. I hear that the clerks still tend them."

The morning sun had risen higher, shortening the shadows around them. Government workers were arriving, carrying briefcases and coffee cups, walking past history they barely noticed anymore.

"You know what I love about Santa Fe?" Gus asked as they headed back toward the Plaza. "How the past and present mix together. Spanish colonial next to American territorial next to modern southwest. Like layers of truth, all visible if you know how to look."

The Plaza filled up quickly with tourists mixing with locals. Gus stopped and pointed eastward where above them all, the Sangre de Cristo Mountains kept their ancient watch over the city where justice and power had danced their complicated dance for over four hundred years.

Sam listened to Gus talk about being a prosecutor, trying to picture his grandfather as a young man, as a young lawyer, but he still wondered if his story about charging the energy company with homicide, with actual murder, was all some sort of dream or story that his grandfather had made up.

"It all seems so cool and peaceful around here," Sam spoke up. "I mean it's a small little town, it doesn't seem like the kind of place where the big energy company would be charged with such a serious crime. It seems like some big Department of Justice prosecutor would be doing this in New York or Washington, DC., but not here." He paused a moment before he added, "It seems like this would be like some huge national news and nobody seems to know about it."

"You make a good point." Gus said and offered no more.

"You were telling me about how you and Phil did it. How did you get the murder charge to stick."

"Here's what made it homicide," Gus explained. "You have three key elements: knowledge, causation, and depraved indifference to human life." He pulled out a piece of paper from his bag and started writing. "First degree murder requires premeditation and specific intent to kill. That was not our case. We were looking at depraved indifference murder and criminally negligent homicide."

"You will need to explain that to me," Sam said.

Gus began to walk him through it. "Depraved indifference murder occurs when someone engages in conduct that creates a grave risk of death, shows depraved indifference to human life, and causes death. I remember Phil handed me the internal memo from Peterson Energy dated 1973, and pointed out that it was their own risk assessment. They had calculated expected mortality rates from particulate emissions. They knew people would die, they put a number on it."

"I argued that it was just statistical modeling and challenged him, playing devil's advocate. I had researched this and told him they did not have specific knowledge of individual deaths."

Sam nodded, "That sounds about right, at least from the crime shows I've seen."

"Yes, but Phil was clever that way. He explained that was where the fraud came in, and he pulled out another document, this one marked with yellow highlights. He pointed out that they didn't just know. They actively concealed the danger. He told me to look at their public statements versus their internal communications. Classic fraudulent concealment."

"I get that," Sam interjected. "But why not just file a civil lawsuit against the company?"

"Good question. Phil explained that criminal charges were better because civil cases drag on for years. The companies can delay, appeal, tie everything up in procedural motions. Meanwhile, people keep dying. But criminal prosecution? I remember his eyes lit up. He said that a criminal case moves quickly. Grand jury, indictment, trial. No shareholders to protect, no quarterly profits to maintain. Just the raw question: did they commit negligent homicide?"

"What's that? Sam asked.

Gus continued. "The elements of criminally negligent homicide are easier to prove. We'd only need to show they failed to perceive a substantial risk that a reasonable person would have perceived.

"Phil liked this theory and pointed out that we had decades of evidence showing that Peterson Energy Company not only perceived the risk—they quantified it. But there was more and he kept going, explaining why this was more than just negligence."

"So, why was it?" Sam wanted to know.

Gus always knew that Sam was intelligent. "What do you think?"

Sam spoke slowly. "The active concealment. They didn't just fail to perceive a risk—they identified it, studied it, and then hid it while continuing to create that risk."

"Now you're thinking like a prosecutor." Gus said. "I remember that Phil pulled out another file and told me to look at the pattern. It said that in1957, their scientists warned about climate change and health impacts. In 1962, they buried the research and fund studies questioning the link. In 1968, there was an internal memo that confirmed increased mortality rates in exposed communities. Finally, in 1969, there was a public statement calling such claims 'unsubstantiated.'"

"So, what's depraved indifference?" Sam asked.

"When you know your actions will result in death, take steps to hide that knowledge, and do it anyway—that's not civil liability. That's homicide."

Gus continued with more. "Phil pointed out that civil law is about money. Making them pay damages, cover medical bills. But I tell you, what we had wasn't about money. It was about holding them criminally accountable for deaths they knew they were causing."

"Sounds a lot like the climate change going on today," Sam said. "So, the burden of proof is higher in criminal cases, right?"

"That's right. Harder to prove, but the impact is greater. Civil penalties are just a cost of doing business to them.

But criminal charges?" Gus smiled grimly. "Well, that gets their attention. That puts their executives at risk of prison time. That makes them face the human cost of their decisions. Criminal penalties can make them change how they do business."

"I remember that Phil pulled out one more document—the death certificate for Maria...Maria Valdez, age nine. He said that this wasn't about statistics anymore. This was about specific victims, specific deaths, specific choices made by specific people who thought they were above the law.

"I remember picking up the death certificate, reading the clinical description of respiratory failure. I asked him how many others. He said there were hundreds just in New Mexico, and thousands across the country."

Gus spoke quietly. "Each one was a person, not a number in a risk assessment model. Each one was a life ended by decisions made in boardrooms by people who thought profit mattered more than people.

"I thought about my corporate law classes in law school and my plans to be a corporate lawyer, about how I would make a living helping companies navigate around regulations, find loopholes, and minimize liability."

"You were going to be a corporate lawyer?" Sam asked.

Gus shook his head without answering. "I told Phil the obvious. That they would fight back hard. 'Of course they will,' he said. 'The rich and powerful always always do. That's why Don Quixote carried a lance.'"

Sam was taken by surprise at his grandfather's mention

of Don Quixote. He wondered what was really going on and whether this was a real story. Humoring the old man, he asked, "How did you respond to that?"

"I asked him what we were going to carry."

"What? You mean, what was your weapon?"

"That's right." Gus stood up and held up his palm. "Phil held up the stack of evidence, all the documents, and said we were going to use the truth, their own words, their own calculations, their own admissions of guilt, all hidden in filing cabinets where they thought no one would ever look."

Sam sat in silence while he attempted to take this all in.

Gus continued, "I asked if he really thought a jury would understand all this? The science, the statistics, the corporate structure. But Phil was adamant that they would understand homicide. He said that they would understand that when you know your actions will kill people, and you do them anyway, that's murder. Everything else is just details. I remember looking at Maria Valdez's death certificate again, at the red dot on Phil's map that marked where she lived and died in the shadow of the Peterson plant's smokestacks."

Sam looked with questioning eyes. "So?"

"Phil handed me one of those yellow legal pads he had and said that we were going to start by building a case to present to the grand jury. We would start with the elements of the crime. Knowledge. Causation. Depraved indifference. We would build it piece by piece, document by document, death by death. We would show that every time they chose profit over people, they were committing murder."

CHAPTER 18

FACT OR FICTION

Gus contacted some old friends the next morning and he and Sam were invited over for dinner that evening. They decided to take a break from camping and booked a room at a small motel on the southern edge of town.

The Ruiz house sat on a hill above Santa Fe, adobe walls glowing pink in the sunset. Elena Ruiz had been Phil's deputy prosecutor before starting her own practice, and her husband Tony had been the office's lead investigator. Now they hosted what Elena called "survivors' dinners" for the old team whenever anyone passed through town.

Their back patio looked out over the city. The air smelled of piñon wood smoke from their chimenea fireplace and something amazing happening to meat on their grill. Sam sat with his legs dangling from the adobe wall, watching lights come on across the valley while the adults caught up over wine.

"Phil was not afraid to prosecute anyone who he felt committed a crime and he brought lots of interesting cases," Tony explained to Sam. "Like the one where the defendant stole Greek artifacts from the Albuquerque Museum and planted a few of them along the banks of the Rio Grande River. He then sold expensive tickets to his archeological expeditions company which would take folks to explore up the river under his novel theory that the ancient Greeks had sailed up the Rio Grande River and, lo and behold, they would find these Greek artifacts along the banks."

"Really? So what happened in that case?" Sam wanted to know.

Tony responded with a smile. "Defendant was convicted of fraud, of course." He then laughed and added, "The jury loved that trial!"

"Oh god, tell Sam about the travelling circus case," Elena said, laughing already at the memory. "The one with Phil and that old elephant."

"The statute clearly covered all forms of transport," Gus protested, but he was grinning. "How were we supposed to know it didn't apply to elephants?"

Tony topped off everyone's wine. "So there's Phil, standing in front of the judge, arguing with a straight face that technically, an elephant qualifies as a commercial vehicle under New Mexico state law."

"Because it was being used to transport goods for profit," Elena added. "He had diagrams. Mathematical calculations about elephant cargo capacity."

"The judge kept trying not to laugh," Gus said. "But Phil was dead serious. Had expert witnesses ready to testify about elephant-based commerce throughout history."

"What happened?" Sam asked.

"Judge threw it out," Tony said. "But not before Phil convinced the circus to upgrade their animal care protocols. Which was what he wanted all along."

"That was Phil's gift," Elena said, her voice softening. "He'd find these crazy legal theories that shouldn't work—"

"Like charging a corporation with homicide..." Tony started to add.

"—but somehow they'd end up changing things. Even when he lost, he won."

In Sam's pocket, the phone was paused in the middle of chapter seven of *Don Quixote*. Sam thought about the way the knight's apparent madness often achieved what sanity couldn't. And then there was the part where the nobles used Don Quixote's outrageous exploits as bawdy entertainment.

"Tell him about the water rights case," Tony said. "The one with the coffee cup demonstration."

Gus groaned. "Oh god, the coffee cups."

"Phil shows up to court with a stack of paper cups," Elena explained, "and starts pouring water between them right there at the prosecutor's table. Trying to demonstrate watershed dynamics to the jury."

"Made a mess," Tony said. "But by god, that jury understood water rights by the end."

"The bailiff tried to stop him," Gus added. "But Phil just worked him into the demonstration. Had him hold cups on the upper tributaries."

The stories flowed like the wine—the defendant who conned investors into believing he had developed the technology to convert lead into marketable amounts of gold, Gus having to measure every window in a hundred-year-old building for a historic preservation fight, and Elena using a Navajo peyote runner as an expert witness in a pharmacy licensing case.

"The thing about Phil," Tony said later, as the night cooled and Elena brought out blankets, "was that he actually believed in the law. Not just as a set of rules, but as a way to make things right."

"Even when making things right meant redefining what the law could do," Elena added.

"Especially then," Gus said quietly.

Sam thought about Don Quixote, who saw the world not as it was but as it should be. Who fought for honor in a world that had forgotten what honor meant. He also thought about how all those people around Don Quixote thought he was simply a crazy old man creating havoc.

"Tell him about the victory garden," Elena said suddenly. "The one Phil planted outside the courthouse."

"Victory garden?" Sam asked.

"During one of the power plant cases," Gus explained.

"Phil decided the clerk's office at the courthouse needed a garden. Said if we were going to fight about air quality, we should grow something that needed clean air to survive."

"The maintenance crew kept removing the plants," Tony said. "Phil kept replanting them. At night. In his suit."

"The district judge finally ordered him to stop," Elena added. "Said it was vandalism."

"So what did he do?"

Gus smiled. "Started bringing potted plants into the courthouse instead. One at a time. Until the clerk's office looked like a greenhouse. Said if they wouldn't let him plant justice outside, he'd grow it inside."

"Did any of the plants survive?" Sam asked.

"Some of them are still there," Elena said. "The clerk's office has a tomato plant that's supposedly from Phil's original garden. They call it the Justice Tomato."

Later, as Gus and Sam were leaving, Elena pulled a small photo album from her bookshelf. "Look at this," she said, opening to a yellowed newspaper clipping inserted among the photos. The picture in the article showed a younger Phil and Gus standing in front of the courthouse. Behind them, barely visible, was a row of small plants pushing up through the hard New Mexico soil.

"Most people thought we were too aggressive, some said we were crazy," Gus said, looking at the photo. "Maybe we were."

"Maybe the world needs a little crazy," Elena replied. "Someone has to grow tomatoes in the desert. Someone has to believe the law can do more than it's done before."

"Someone has to fight windmills," Sam said quietly.

They all looked at Sam, and he felt himself blush. But Elena just smiled.

"Exactly," she said.

Riding back to their hotel, the city lights below looked like fallen stars. Sam thought about Phil in his suit, planting seeds in the dark, believing something could grow in unlikely soil. About all these people who'd followed him into battle after battle, not necessarily because they thought they would win, but because they believed the fight itself was worth something.

When they arrived back at their hotel, the pair sat quietly on the small patio in front of their room. Sam listened to the part of Don Quixote where the Duke and Duchess encountered the knight and his squire. He read aloud from his phone:

And so the Duke and Duchess, with their courtiers and servants, made great sport of Don Quixote and Sancho Panza, devising elaborate jests and pranks, treating their quest as mere entertainment for their idle hours. For it pleased them to see a knight so earnest in his delusions, never suspecting that perhaps the truest madness lay in those who made light of sacred causes.

Gus nodded slowly in the light emanating from the open door. "You know, that's exactly what Peterson's corporate executives did with Phil at first. Their lawyers invited him over to discuss his investigation, treated his concerns as a kind of amusing distraction. 'That quixotic prosecutor with his environmental theories and talk of criminal prosecution,' they'd say, laughing behind their hands."

"Until he got too close to the truth?"

"Right. Just like with Don Quixote—the nobles found him entertaining until his 'madness' started making too much sense. The companies were happy to humor Phil until he started producing real evidence, real documents. Then suddenly it wasn't so funny anymore."

"So they stopped laughing and started fighting."

"The powerful always prefer to treat truth-tellers as jesters," Gus said, putting down the magazine he had been reading. "It's easier than facing what they're really saying. Until suddenly the jester proves he's been serious all along—then they show their true colors."

Outside, the stars wheeled overhead while they considered how little has changed since Cervantes' time—how those with power still preferred to laugh at those who challenged them, until laughter was no longer enough.

On the phone in Sam's pocket, Don Quixote waited to continue his own impossible quest. But somehow, after the night's stories, his madness seemed less mad. Or maybe, Sam was finally beginning to understand what Dr. Fitz had meant about the difference between seeing what is and seeing what should be.

CHAPTER 19

NEW MEXICO TO ARIZONA

Gus and Sam left Santa Fe as the sun rose over the Sangre de Cristos, taking the back roads west. Through Los Alamos, where atomic history sits uneasily among the piñon pines, the old bikes climbed steadily into the Jemez Mountains.

They rode past Jemez Springs, where hot springs steamed in the morning cool, then Cuba, where ranching met reservation land. The landscape opened up, each mesa telling its own story in layers of red and orange stone.

They crossed into Navajo Nation near Nageezi and the character of the land shifted subtly. As they passed Pueblo Pintado, Gus pointed toward the ancient Chacoan ruins. "It's good to be reminded that these civilizations were older than European memory."

The bikes maintained their steady rhythm while sacred mountains appeared and receded on the horizon.

"Different sense of time out here," Gus observed during a stop in Crownpoint. "Measured in geology rather than years."

They stopped for fuel in Gallup, where trading post signs advertised Navajo rugs and turquoise jewelry. Gus pointed out the ancient trade routes that paralleled the highway, paths that had connected civilizations long before cars and trucks marked distance in miles.

Leading the way, Gus turned unexpectedly onto a road headed northeast toward a place called Church Rock. Accustomed to these unannounced detours, Sam followed. He noted how the morning sun cast long shadows across the red earth, while the distant mesas rose like ancient guardians. Gus led them to a stopping point overlooking what seemed like an ordinary arroyo.

"July 16, 1979," Gus said, as he dismounted and removed his helmet. "The worst radioactive spill in U.S. history happened right here. Worse than Three Mile Island, but hardly anyone outside New Mexico knows about it."

Sam looked at the peaceful-seeming landscape. "What happened?"

"The United Nuclear Corporation's uranium mill tailings dam broke. Released ninety million gallons of acidic, radioactive water and eleven hundred tons of radioactive mill wastes into the Pipeline Arroyo." Gus pointed to where the dry streambed winded through the landscape. "Flowed right into the Rio Puerco. The same water people used for their livestock, their crops, their families."

They walked to the edge of the overlook. A raven circled overhead, its shadow crossing the contaminated ground below.

"The company knew the dam was unstable," Gus continued. "Their own engineers warned them. But fixing it would have cut into profits." He paused. "Just like the patterns Phil found in his case against the energy company. Same story, different poison."

"What happened to the people?"

"Navajo families were wading in the water before anyone warned them. Livestock died. Cancer rates soared. The contamination spread eighty miles downstream." Gus kicked a stone and watched it tumble down the slope. A train whistle echoed across the desert. Gus turned and pointed in its direction. "Probably carrying coal and uranium from mines that are still operating."

"Phil used to cite this case all the time," Gus said. "Said it showed how companies calculate risk against profit, how they decide whose lives matter and whose don't." He looked toward the distant mountains of the Navajo. "The cleanup's still not complete, more than forty years later. The land remembers, even if most people have forgotten."

They mounted their motorcycles to continue toward Flagstaff, leaving behind a place where the earth held secrets measured in half-lives and broken promises, while ahead, the Arizona desert waited with its own stories of environmental reckoning.

"Watch how the land changes," Gus's voice came

through the intercom as they crossed into Arizona. "Every color means something different. Red iron, white calcium, black volcanic glass."

The pair stopped at an overlook about halfway between Gallup and Flagstaff. Gus pointed to the south towards Arizona's White Mountains. He told Sam that even after twelve years, the landscape bore the scars of the Wallow Fire—at 538,000 acres, it was the largest fire in Arizona's history.

"If you could see the tree line," Gus said to Sam, pointing to the horizon. "You can still see exactly where the fire stopped. Nature takes generations to heal from something like that."

Sam removed his helmet to look. "What caused it?"

"Officially? An abandoned campfire. But that was just the spark." Gus took off his sunglasses and stretched his back. He looked again towards the mountains. "The real cause was decades of rising temperatures, prolonged drought, bark beetle infestations—all made worse by climate change." He continued. "The fire burned for six weeks and destroyed hundreds of buildings, forced thousands to evacuate. Cost more than $100 million to fight." He turned to Sam. "You know what my friend Phil would probably say? He'd say every acre burned there was connected to those business decisions he tried to challenge. Every dead tree was evidence in a case about how the fossil fuel companies are responsible for what climate change is doing to the world. A case that's still waiting to be tried."

The wind picked up and carried the scent of pine toward

them, while overhead, the clouds cast shadows across the landscape.

"The companies knew this was coming," Gus said quietly.

"What are you talking about?" Sam wanted to know.

Gus answered in a low voice, almost talking to himself. "Their own scientists predicted it—the man-made carbon emissions that have heated up the atmosphere, created the greenhouse effect, heated up the oceans, the globe, longer fire seasons, more intense burns, whole ecosystems changed forever. But they have buried the evidence, just like they buried everything else that might have made a difference." He paused for a second and then added, "The energy companies knew, and so did the politicians who are in their pockets."

Without saying more, Gus turned and walked to the bikes. He slowly put on his helmet, gloves, and sunglasses. "Onward ho," he said to his young partner. Sam had learned quite a bit about how his grandfather communicated his thoughts during their journey. He would state a fact or make an observation, and if he felt there was not any more to say right then, he would simply move on. The two mounted up and continued.

The San Francisco Peaks finally appeared on the horizon like a mirage, their slopes dark with ponderosa pine. Flagstaff sat in their shadow. It was a mountain town that felt more like it was in Colorado than in Arizona.

Sam rewound the audio back to where the narrator was describing the aftermath of the windmill fight—how

Don Quixote lay battered but unbowed, still insisting that the giants had been transformed into windmills by an evil enchanter. Sam thought about Phil's map in the district attorney's office, all those red strings connecting deaths to decisions. About how something could be both real and impossible to prove, like rain that never reaches the ground.

Hours later they found a campground at the edge of the Coconino National Forest, where the desert meets the largest continuous ponderosa pine forest in North America. After setting up their tents and gear, Sam lay flat on his sleeping bag outside his tent, overcome with an exhaustion caused by the heat and wind of the open road. Gus received a phone call and went into his tent. Through the tent walls Sam could hear his grandfather on the phone, his voice a low murmur as he talked to Phil or someone who knew him. Sam remembered how earlier, he had told him more specifics about the case—the additional internal memos and risk assessments, about companies that counted deaths like other businesses counted inventory shrinkage. Normal business expenses. "Could that really be true?" Sam had asked himself silently.

"What does a grand jury do?" Sam asked when Gus returned.

"In a nutshell, in a criminal case, the police conduct an investigation by gathering the evidence. They also talk to witnesses. Then they take what they have found to the prosecutor who decides if he or she thinks there is enough evidence to find them guilty beyond a reasonable doubt. If so, they take the case to a grand jury which issues an indictment based on whether they find there is probable cause the crime was committed."

"What's probable cause?" Sam asked. "I thought you said proof beyond a reasonable doubt in a criminal case?"

"For an indictment, the prosecutor has a lower burden of proof. Probable cause means if the evidence is more than fifty percent that the crime was committed. It's a lower bar because the indictment is just the charging document. At trial, the prosecutor has to prove the case beyond a reasonable doubt. Does this make sense?"

"Yeah, I guess so."

Gus continued with his quick summary of criminal law. "In many if not most cases there is a plea bargain, but often times a case will go to trial. That is by either a bench trial where the judge decides the case or by a jury trial, where twelve people, the jurors, hear and see the evidence and must all agree that the prosecutor has proved the case beyond a reasonable doubt. If so, then they find the defendant guilty. If not, then it's a not guilty verdict."

"So, you were talking about a grand jury before. What exactly is that? I mean is that different from a trial jury?"

"Good question," Gus responded. "A grand jury is a group of normally twelve citizens who reside in the locality where the crime was committed, who look at evidence gathered by the police and prosecutors and decide if there is probable cause to hand down an indictment against the accused person."

"What's an indictment?" Sam asked again.

"It's the charging document against the person. If the grand jury decides there is probable cause that the person committed the crime then they hand down the indictment. As I mentioned, it's a lower burden of proof than a jury decision, which must be unanimous and, like I said, beyond a reasonable doubt. Also, in a grand jury proceeding, there is no defense attorney and no cross examining of the evidence. It simply shows that there is enough evidence to charge the person with the crime. The grand jury is often used in big complex cases and the indictment is often placed under seal, which means that no one in the public knows about it. Once the indictment is unsealed by the prosecutor then the case goes public and the evidence is brought out in open court for all to see."

"And is that what happened in that New Mexico case?" Sam asked.

"That's right, sort of. We put together the case against the Peterson Coal Company charging them with negligent homicide."

"So, what happened? Did the case go to a regular trial? Did you win?"

Without answering, Gus looked down before he continued. "I remember, it was 1984, and we were meeting to present the case to the grand jury in Santa Fe. Twelve citizens along with two alternates sat in worn wooden chairs, their faces showing varying degrees of skepticism and curiosity. Phil had spent the morning explaining the basics of criminally negligent homicide. Then it was time for the evidence."

"Were you in the room? Were you part of all this?" Sam asked.

"Yes. We presented all the evidence I talked about. The Peterson Energy internal memo from 1957, about continued coal burning operations that would lead to significant accumulation of carbon dioxide in the atmosphere resulting in temperature increases and adverse health impacts in exposed populations. Even way back then Peterson Energy knew what burning fossil fuels would do to our air, our climate, our children. But knowledge isn't enough for criminal liability, so we had to have them look at what they did with this knowledge.

"There was the 1968 mortality study, which was a document that showed they didn't just know in theory. They measured death rates in communities downwind of their plants. They calculated excess mortality. They put numbers to the cost of doing business."

"How did the grand jury react to all this stuff? Sam asked.

"I remember a man in the back—retired military, crew cut still rigid—leaned forward and asked if we were saying they knew people would die? I remember Phil looked right at him and said, 'I'm saying they counted how many would die.'

"We had an easel where we'd mounted a map similar to the one in his office and explained that each red dot represented a death that was directly linked to Peterson Energy's emissions. Each string connected to a corporate decision that allowed those deaths to continue.

"We distributed a set of documents—internal communications about suppressing research, redirecting studies, hiding evidence.

"I remember Phil telling them that all this wasn't negligence, it was a choice. When you know your actions will result in death, when you take steps to hide that knowledge, when you continue those actions anyway—that's depraved indifference to human life.

"There was a teacher in the room who asked if all those people, the ones who died... did their families know why."

"We explained that some suspected, but most had been told that their loved ones died from natural causes. Cancer. Respiratory failure. Heart disease. Phil then told them that they didn't know that a corporation calculated the probability of their deaths and decided the profit was worth the cost."

"So, what was it like, to be there?"

"We'd prepared testimony from epidemiologists, climate scientists, medical experts, and I remember a witness we used. She was an elderly woman supporting herself with a cane. I remember her name. Mrs. Ann Running Horse. Her husband James had died three years prior after living his entire life in the shadow of Peterson Energy's largest plant. She told them that her husband never smoked. She said he never drank. Worked his land, took care of his family. Then one day he couldn't breathe right. Then he couldn't breathe at all.

"She told them that the doctors showed them the spots on his lungs. Said it was cancer. But he knew. He'd watch that smoke from their towers drift over their land year after year. He knew what was killing him.

"At the end, I remember that Phil picked up the 1957 memo again and told them that the company can't claim they didn't know. They couldn't claim it was an accident. They knew. They calculated. They concealed. And people died."

Sam sat up. "Wow. That's pretty heavy stuff."

"Phil told them that we wanted them to do what the law requires. If they found probable cause that Peterson Energy caused deaths through criminal negligence and depraved indifference to human life, then they should indict them. Not for breaking regulations. Not for civil violations. For homicide.

"I remember one of them, it was that military man, spoke up again and said that they would fight back. A company that big, with that much money.

"Phil agreed, but that for once, they would have to fight in the open. No more hiding evidence. No more burying truth. They would have to explain in a criminal court why knowing your actions will kill people isn't murder."

Sam was fully engaged. "So, then what happened next?"

"Well, we presented the final exhibit—a list of names. Every person we could document who had died from causes linked to Peterson Energy's emissions. Phil told them to read their names. Look at their pictures. Remember that each red dot on that map was a person, a life, a family destroyed. Then to ask themselves that if this wasn't criminal homicide, then what was?"

"That is pretty incredible story," Sam said. "It sounds a lot like what is going on today. Really, I mean the big energy corporations causing the climate change that's burning this whole place up. Why do you suppose everyone is just letting it happen?"

Sam pulled out Dr. Fitz's copy of *Don Quixote*, its margins crowded with his cramped handwriting. Near the windmill passage, he'd written: "Question—Is madness seeing what isn't there, or seeing what others refuse to acknowledge?"

Lightning flickered in the distance and Sam imagined them illuminating the silhouettes of refineries on the eastern horizon. Their flares burned against the dark like tiny suns. In Sam's ears, Sancho was trying to convince Don Quixote that the windmills had always been windmills, that there were no giants, that he was chasing shadows.

But were they shadows? Sam thought about what Gus had told him about the evidence—decades of knowledge hidden in filing cabinets, scientists' warnings buried under lawyers' denials. Giants disguising themselves as ordinary machines, counting on everyone being too sane, and too comfortable, to see them for what they really were.

A few minutes of quiet was interrupted when Gus's

phone rang. He looked at it and then stepped into his tent to talk to the caller.

Sam turned over and opened his notebook—the one he had started keeping after their first night on the road. Under his earlier entries about landscape and weather, Sam wrote:

Don Quixote isn't crazy because he sees giants. He's crazy because he thinks he can defeat them alone.

Phil wasn't crazy either. He had evidence, documents, proof. But maybe the real enchanter wasn't turning giants into windmills—maybe it was turning deaths into statistics, people into numbers, murder into math.

The tent flap opened and Gus stepped out, slipping his phone into his pocket. He looked at Sam's notebook but didn't ask what he was writing.

"Phil was excited about meeting you," he said, sitting down beside Sam. "He wanted to hear what you thought about his old windmills."

"Did he really think he could win?" Sam asked. "Against the companies?"

Gus was quiet for a moment, watching the lightning dance between clouds. "You know what's interesting about Don Quixote? Everyone remembers that he lost the fight with the windmills. They forget that he got back up and kept riding."

"But what's the point of fighting if you know you'll lose?"

"Who says they won?" He nodded toward the refineries on the horizon. "Look around. People are finally seeing them for what they are. It just took a few mad knights to point them out first."

Sam thought about Mrs. Henderson in her office, with all her safe harbors mapped out in different colored pens. About Dr. Fitz asking if Sam was more afraid of the deep water or the safe harbor. About Don Quixote, who saw the world not as it was, but as it should be.

"In the book," Sam said, "Sancho follows Don Quixote even though he knows his master is crazy. Even though he sees windmills instead of giants. Why?"

Gus smiled. "Maybe because it's better to fight windmills for the right reasons than to ignore giants for the wrong ones."

After the two had eaten and settled in for the evening, Sam dialed back to the story. In his earbuds, Don Quixote was mounting his horse again, battered but undefeated, ready for the next battle. Behind Sam and Gus, the storm was moving closer, and he imagined the refinery flares burned brighter against the darkening sky.

Sam added one more line to his notebook:

Sometimes the crazy choice and the right choice are the same thing. The trick is finding people crazy enough to help you fight anyway.

The first drops of rain began to fall, the desert finally accepting the storm. Sam sat there with his grandfather watching it come. He thought that somewhere in California, an old knight was waiting to tell about the injustices he'd seen, and the battles he'd fought, and why some quests are worth everything they cost.

CHAPTER 20

ARIZONA TO CALIFORNIA

S am and Gus left Flagstaff before dawn. The air was mountain-cold as their headlights cut through darkness. As they descended from the Colorado Plateau, the temperature rose with each mile. By the time they got close to the California state line, the sun had turned the world into a furnace.

The pair stopped at a rest area next to a McDonalds just outside of Kingman, Arizona. To Sam it seemed like the kind of nowhere place that existed only because humans needed breaks between real destinations. He sat at a weathered picnic table in some shade, *Don Quixote* playing in his earbuds, while Gus checked the fluids on the bikes.

The narrator had reached the part where Sancho begins to doubt his master's stories of glory—all those giants that looked suspiciously like windmills, all those armies that seemed to be sheep.

Sancho is talking to his wife, saying: 'I sometimes think that all these things my master speaks of—the battles, the giants, the armies—perhaps they are all fantasies, wind and lies. Yet I have seen them with my own eyes, though they appeared to me as something else entirely.'

Sam thought about the stories from the other night's dinner, about Phil's crusading victories, other amusing cases, and clever legal maneuvers. They'd felt inspiring in the warm glow of Elena's patio lights, but out there in the harsh desert sun, something didn't add up. They were almost too amazing to be true.

Sam pulled out his phone and did what he should have done days ago—searched for news articles about Phil Stone and the Peterson Energy case. There wasn't much. A few local newspaper clips, mostly buried in archives. Nothing about grand jury indictments or criminal charges. Nothing about a groundbreaking homicide case against energy companies.

"Having doubts?" Gus asked, wiping his hands on a rag. He'd been watching Sam scroll through his phone.

"These stories you're telling me," Sam said. "About Phil and the case. Did that really happen? I mean, the way you were telling them?"

Gus sat down across from him, the picnic table creaking under his weight. "What do you think?"

"I think…" Sam paused the audiobook. "I think maybe

you're doing what Don Quixote does. Taking something small and turning it into something grand. You know, exaggerating things..."

"Interesting theory." He pulled out his water bottle, took a long drink. Behind him, a truck's air brakes hissed in the parking lot. "What makes you say that?"

"There's nothing online about the case. No record of any grand jury indictment for homicide against energy companies. Nothing about Phil except a few small mentions in local papers about other cases." Sam met his eyes. "If it was such a big deal, wouldn't there be more?"

"Ah." He nodded slowly. "So if you can't find it on Google, it didn't happen?"

"That's not what I meant."

"No?" He looked out at the mountains. "When Don Quixote told his stories of glory, everyone assumed he was crazy because they couldn't see what he saw. But does that make him wrong?"

"It makes him delusional," Sam said. "He literally attacks windmills thinking they're evil giants."

"Does he?" Gus turned back to Sam. "Or does he see something in those windmills that everyone else has learned not to see?"

"Now you sound like Dr. Fitz."

"Good teacher, that one." The old man smiled. "But you haven't answered my question. What do you think Phil saw when he looked at those power plants? What did he see in those internal memos and death certificates that everyone else had learned to ignore?"

Sam thought about the red strings on Phil's map, connecting dots that everyone else saw as separate points. About how sometimes patterns only become visible when someone is crazy enough to look for them. He thought about past damage done and about the present global climate crisis.

"But the case failed," Sam said. "Didn't it? That's why there's no record."

"Did it?" He pulled something from his wallet—an old, creased newspaper clipping. It showed a younger version of him standing with Phil outside the Santa Fe courthouse. The headline was barely legible: "AG's Office Launches Investigation into Peterson Energy Operations."

"That's all that got printed?"

"That's all that could get printed. It was a secret grand jury and the indictment was under seal." He carefully folded the clipping away. "Sometimes, Sam, the story isn't in what makes the papers. It's in what gets kept out of them."

"So what really happened?"

"What happened is what always happens when someone points at giants that everyone else has agreed to call windmills. They push back." He stood up, stretched. "But that doesn't mean they weren't giants."

"That's not an answer."

"No," he agreed. "But maybe that's because you're asking the wrong question. Don Quixote isn't about whether the giants were real. It's about what happens when someone decides to fight them anyway."

In his pocket, Sam's phone showed zero search results

for "Phil Stone homicide case energy companies." But Gus had said that the photo in his wallet had been real. He had told him that the map in Phil's office had been real. The death certificates had been real. But maybe he was dreaming things, like riding in the desert. Mirages.

"We should get back on the road," Gus said. "Still have a lot of miles to cover."

Sam put his earbuds back in, started the book again. Don Quixote was explaining to Sancho how the knight's cause was measured:

Listen well, Sancho, for this is the heart of knight-errantry: the worth of our cause is not measured by its victory or defeat, but by its justice. A knight's glory lies not in winning, but in whether the fight itself was worth the fighting. For it is better to fail in a noble cause than to triumph in a lesser one. The world may call us mad for battling giants that they name as windmills, but what matters is not their laughter, but the truth we serve.

When they reached the California line the Mojave Desert stretched before them, vast and implacable. Sam noticed several signs that warned of extreme heat and advised travelers to carry extra water. The temperature climbed to 90 degrees before noon. Through their helmet intercoms, Gus reminded Sam to keep drinking water at every stop.

The landscape seemed alive with heat—Joshua trees twisted like sculptures, volcanic peaks rising from endless flats, mirages shimmering on the horizon. But it was the relentless sun that occupied Sam's thoughts; it felt different from the sun he knew back east—more intense, more dangerous.

At a rest stop outside Needles where even the wind felt like a blast furnace, Sam watched heat waves distort the air above the asphalt. The Colorado River was visible in the distance, its water level shockingly low, exposing pale bathtub rings on the canyon walls that marked where the water used to reach.

Gus passed Sam another water bottle, insisting on hydration in the brutal heat. "This drought isn't natural," he said, gesturing toward the diminished river. "At least, not entirely."

Sam wiped sweat from his face. "Climate change?"

"Climate change engineered by people who knew exactly what they were doing." Gus leaned against his bike, which was too hot to sit on. "Remember those documents Phil found? The internal memos from the energy companies? They had climate models from the 1970s that predicted exactly this—increasing temperatures, prolonged droughts, water scarcity in the West."

A dust devil spun across the parking lot, picking up trash before dissipating.

"Their own scientists told them burning fossil fuels would alter the climate. Told them it would lead to exactly what we're seeing—hotter temperatures, changing precipitation patterns, more extreme weather events. And what did they do with that information?"

"Buried it," Sam said, remembering Phil's case.

"Worse than buried it. They funded disinformation campaigns to create doubt about the very science their own researchers had confirmed." Gus looked toward the shrinking river. "Meanwhile, they built their oil platforms higher to account for the rising sea levels they publicly denied were coming."

A family pulled into the rest stop. Sam noticed that the children looked wilted in the back seat and the parents' faces were tight with the strain of traveling through such heat.

"Look around you," Gus continued. "Lake Mead down to historic lows. Colorado River so depleted they're fighting over every drop. California wildfires burning hotter and longer each year. And it's not just here—droughts in Africa, floods in Asia, heat waves in Europe. All predicted by models these companies had decades ago."

"But proving they caused it legally..."

"Like I said before, that was the challenge Phil took on. Showing that they knew, that they hid that knowledge, and that people died as a result." Gus drank from his own water bottle. "These aren't natural disasters anymore. They're corporate decisions playing out over decades, with the costs pushed onto everyone else while the profits stay private."

They mounted their bikes, the heat rising in waves from the asphalt. Ahead, the Mojave Desert stretched toward the horizon, its harshness intensified by human choices made in distant boardrooms long ago.

Sam could not help but think about Phil's case again, about companies that knew their actions would change the climate but chose profit anyway. He thought about the internal memos that calculated deaths against dividends.

The temperature hit 95 degrees as they approached Barstow. The desert seemed to be trying to tell them something, its harsh beauty a warning about fragility and consequence. Sam remembered the evidence Gus described—decades of hiding knowledge and years of burying the truth, while the world grew hotter degree by degree.

They found a motel in Barstow—it was too hot for camping. In their room, after the air conditioning had driven the desert from their bones, Sam sat on the edge of his bed, staring at his phone—at the messages from his father about internship opportunities "still available if you end this motorcycle nonsense," at Ellen's Instagram showing her campus life at Princeton, at news alerts about another environmental disaster somewhere.

"What's the point of all this?" he finally said, tossing the phone aside. "Riding across the country to visit someone I never met, to hear about a case that failed, to see damage that nobody's fixing. We're just... tourists passing through other people's problems."

Gus looked up from the map he'd been studying. "Having doubts?"

"More than doubts. This whole trip—what's it actually accomplishing? We see environmental disasters, you tell me stories about Phil, I listen to Don Quixote, and nothing changes. The giants are still winning."

Sam paced the small room. "Maybe Dad's right. Maybe I

should just take the internship, follow the normal path, stop pretending I can make any difference."

Gus was quiet for a moment. "You know what Don Quixote says to Sancho when they're both beaten and exhausted? *'The road is always better than the inn.'* He means the journey itself has value, even when the destination disappoints."

"But what's the value in this journey? Just seeing how bad things are?"

"The value is in what you're learning to see." Gus sat beside him. "When I started working with Phil, I felt the same way. The case seemed impossible, the opposition too powerful, the damage already done. I wanted to quit, go back to Virginia, take a corporate law job."

"What stopped you?"

"Phil took me to the home of a family whose child had died from pollution-related illness. Not to manipulate me, but to remind me that our legal theories and evidence weren't abstractions—they were about real people, real consequences." Gus looked at Sam. "This journey isn't just about seeing problems. It's about learning to see connections, to understand how they all fit together."

"But we're not fixing anything. We're just... witnesses."

"Every movement for change begins with witnesses. People who see clearly, who tell others what they've seen, who refuse to look away." Gus picked up Sam's phone. "That internship your father's offering—it'll still be there when we get back, if that's what you choose. But this chance to see the country through different eyes, to understand Phil's battle from the inside—that won't come again."

Sam was quiet, considering. Outside their window, the California night was alive with distant winds.

"There's another quote from Don Quixote I've always loved," Gus said. "*Take care, sir, cried Sancho. Those things over there are not giants but windmills.*' And Don Quixote replied, '*You can see how little you know about adventures.*'"

"You think this is an adventure?" Sam asked.

"I think adventures rarely look like adventures while you're in them. Usually they look like hardship, like doubt, like moments when continuing forward seems impossible." Gus stood up and then returned to his map. "But looking back, they're the times that made everything else make sense."

The wind picked up, promising another bout of challenging riding the next day. But somewhere in the sound, Sam began to hear something else—not just noise, but a kind of distant music, like the sound of a story still being written.

"Do you think it's too late?" he asked. "To really do something about what they have done to the climate?"

Gus looked up from his road maps. "Phil used to say that as long as there's truth to be told, it's never too late to tell it."

"But telling isn't enough anymore, is it?"

"No," Gus agreed. "But it's where action starts. Someone has to be willing to fight battles that seem already lost."

Through their window, the desert shimmered in the late afternoon heat, while somewhere in Sam's mind, a decision began to take shape like some distant mountain emerging from haze.

CHAPTER 21

CALIFORNIA

They left Barstow before dawn, trying to cross the Mojave before the worst heat hit. The old BMWs' headlights cut through darkness as the desert slowly revealed itself in shades of gray and purple. By sunrise, they were climbing out of the basin, the temperature dropping as they gained elevation.

"Watch the bikes on these grades," Gus's voice came through the intercom. "Altitude affects the mixture. They'll run rich until we adjust the carbs."

The transformation from desert to forest happened gradually, then suddenly. First scattered pines appeared, then denser stands, until they were riding through corridors of green. The air grew thick with the scent of warm bark and resin.

They stopped at a turnout for Gus to adjust the carburetors. Below them, the desert they crossed stretched to the horizon. Above, the road wound toward the national forest.

"First time I saw a sequoia," Gus said, making fine adjustments to Sam's bike, "I understood why people used to think there were gods in trees. Some of these were already ancient when Rome was young."

The bikes ran better after the adjustment, their old engines adapting to the thinner air. Gus and Sam climbed higher, the road grew tighter, until they rounded a bend and there they were—the first real giants, their trunks wider than their motorcycles were long.

They found a Forest Service campground tucked among the big trees. While setting up their tents, Sam noticed how small their bikes looked, how all human things seem diminished in this company. The sequoias rose like pillars holding up the sky, their bark glowing red-gold in the setting sun.

"Think about it," Gus said as they heated their dinner on the camp stove. "These trees were here before any of our stories began. Before Don Quixote, before corporations, before any of our big human schemes. And they're still here, telling their own kind of truth."

As dusk settled among the sequoias, they noticed smoke from another campfire drifting through the trees. Their neighbor, a man who introduced himself as Ernie, walked over with a pot of coffee to share. His weathered face and quiet manner suggested someone used to listening more than talking.

"These old ones," he said, gesturing at the massive sequoias, "they remind me of the elders back home. Always watching, always teaching, if you know how to listen." He settled near their fire, pouring coffee into the cups they offered.

"You're Navajo?" Gus asked.

Ernie nodded. "Diné. Been coming here for thirty years. These trees, they help me remember what my grandfather taught me about being a warrior."

Sam leaned forward. "What did he teach you?"

"He said there are many ways to be a warrior. Some fight with weapons, some with words, some with wisdom." Ernie sipped his coffee. "But the true warrior fights for something bigger than himself. For the balance between people and the earth, between what we need and what we take."

The firelight caught his face as he continued. "Mother Earth, she's patient. Like these sequoias. But she notices what we do. The poisons we put in her water, the scars we leave on her skin. A warrior's job is to protect this balance, to speak for those who cannot speak—the trees, the waters, the creatures who share this land."

"How do you fight that battle?" Sam asked, thinking about Phil's legal wars, about his own uncertain path.

"Some fight in courtrooms, some in council meetings, some by teaching the old ways to the young. My grandfather would say the weapon matters less than the heart behind it." Ernie looked up at the stars appearing between the sequoia branches. "But first, you have to learn to listen. To the land, to the waters, to these old ones who've seen so much."

They sat in silence for a while, listening to the night sounds of the forest, to the wind in the sequoias' high branches.

"You know what else my grandfather said about warriors?" Ernie added softly. "That the strongest ones don't fight against something—they fight for something. For balance, for justice, for the seventh generation yet to come."

Before returning to his camp, Ernie shared one last thought. "These trees, they've survived fire, drought, human greed. They're still here, still teaching. Maybe that's the greatest warrior lesson—patience and persistence. Standing your ground, like they do, and letting your truth grow deep roots."

After he left, Sam and Gus sat with his words, while around them, the ancient sequoias kept their vigil, warriors in their own right.

CHAPTER 22

SEQUOIA

D awn among the sequoias was a gradual affair, as light filtered down through ancient branches. They packed their bikes in the cool mountain air, the engines' sound muffled by the forest's density. As they descended from the Sierra Nevada, the landscape transformed with each thousand feet of elevation lost.

The big trees gave way to smaller pines, then oak woodlands, then finally the vast Central Valley spread before them. The temperature rose as they dropped into agricultural country, where the geometric patterns of orchards and row crops replaced the wild symmetry of the forest.

"Different kind of industry here," Gus's voice came through the intercom as they passed massive agricultural operations. "Corporate farms, most of them. The small family farms are mostly gone now."

They crossed the valley floor on secondary roads, passing

through small towns that seemed to exist solely to service the surrounding fields. Sam watched the workers bent over strawberry rows in the heat.

The coastal range appeared as a blue line on the horizon, promising cooler air. As they climbed the smaller mountains, the first hints of sea breeze cut through the valley heat. They began to see artichoke fields, then more strawberry operations, the crops changing with the cooling influence of the Pacific.

Watsonville appeared in the valley below them, surrounded by fields and processing plants. The air carried the scent of ocean, mixed with the smell of ripening berries. They stopped at a roadside stand where workers were selling strawberries fresh from the surrounding fields.

"When I first went to visit Phil," Gus said, "he had moved to California and talked about how the big agricultural companies were just like the energy companies—treating the land as something to be used up, the workers as disposable parts in their profit machine."

The late afternoon sun turned the fields to gold, while ahead, the first hints of coastal fog suggested the Pacific's proximity. The old BMWs had carried them from desert to mountain to valley to coast, each landscape telling its own story about power, about use, about change.

They stopped in Watsonville for a late lunch. Sam watched his grandfather check both bikes with the same methodical care he'd shown for thousands of miles. All those stories about Phil, about justice and fighting corruption—were they memories or myths? Truth or teaching tools?

"Almost there," Gus said, adjusting his mirrors.

The final stretch took them up Highway 1, with the Pacific appearing and disappearing around each curve. Fog started to gather, first as wisps, then as solid banks that shrouded the coast. The temperature dropped twenty degrees in as many miles.

Sam thought more about the different stories Gus had told him along the way—Phil in the courtroom, the garden he kept replanting, the case that seemed impossible until it wasn't. Like Don Quixote's tales of knight-errantry and enchantments, they hovered between reality and allegory, truth and teaching.

As the two crossed the Golden Gate Bridge, the fog was rolling in off the Pacific transforming San Francisco into something dreamlike and indistinct. They had been riding since dawn, pushing through the last stretch of California as if Gus was racing something Sam couldn't see.

Gus led them up into the Presidio, where cypress trees emerged from the mist like ancient sentinels. The bike's engine echoed off old military buildings until they finally stopped in front of a small stone chapel. Other vehicles were already parked outside—some cars with New Mexico plates.

"We're meeting Phil here?" Sam asked, as he pulled off his helmet.

Gus didn't answer immediately. He was staring at the chapel door, where a small group of people had gathered. Sam recognized Elena and Tony from Santa Fe, both in black.

Then Sam saw the flowers. The portrait easel. The gentle way people were greeting each other.

"Granddad?"

"Phil died three days ago," he said quietly. "Heart attack in his garden. He was tending his tomato plants when it happened."

The fog swirled around them, carrying the salt smell of the ocean. In his backpack, Don Quixote waited at the chapter Sam had been saving for when he met Phil- the part where the knight finally confronts his greatest challenge.

"You knew," Sam said. It wasn't a question. "This whole time."

"Phil's wife Rachael called after we left Virginia to tell me that he was in declining health." He was still staring at the chapel. "Phil had been sick for a while. Asked me to bring him something. Said he had a story that needed keeping."

Sam's throat felt tight. "Why didn't you tell me?"

"Because you needed to hear his story while it was still alive. While it was still about the fight, not the ending." He finally looked at Sam. "While it could still teach you what you needed to learn."

Rachael spotted the two of them. She walked over, carrying something wrapped in cloth.

"Gus," she said, hugging him. "You made it." She turned to Sam. "And you must be Sam. Phil was so looking forward to meeting you."

"He knew I was coming?"

"Of course." She smiled through tears. "Gus called him the night you decided to make the trip. Phil said it was perfect—one last chance to teach someone about fighting for justice."

She handed Gus the cloth-wrapped package. "He wanted you to have this. Said you'd know what to do with it."

Gus unwrapped it carefully. It was Phil's original map of New Mexico, the one with all the red strings connecting deaths to decisions. The strings had faded, but they were still visible—a web of truth that someone had finally been brave enough to see.

"Classic Phil," Rachael said softly. "Still teaching, even now."

Inside the chapel, people were beginning to take their seats. Sam could see more familiar faces from the photos in the album Elena had showed him in Santa Fe—older now, but still recognizable. Phil's old team, gathered one last time.

"I spent this whole trip wanting to meet him," Sam said. "Thinking about what I'd ask."

"You did meet him," Gus replied. "Through every story, every mile. Through the truth he wasn't afraid to tell." He looked down at the map. "Sometimes the most important meetings aren't the ones that happen in person."

Rachael touched Sam's arm. "Come on. People should hear about your journey. About how Phil's story is still traveling, still teaching."

They walked toward the chapel as the fog parted just enough to let through a shaft of sunlight. Sam thought about all the moments of the trip that suddenly made new sense—Gus's urgency, his need to tell the story right, his insistence that some quests matter even if they end in defeat.

Inside Sam's backpack, Don Quixote waited at his own ending—one Sam had not yet reached, but now understood differently. It wasn't just about a mad knight fighting imaginary giants. It was about how stories survive their tellers, how truth outlives both victory and defeat.

"You know what Phil said when I told him you were reading *Don Quixote*?" Rachael asked as Sam reached the chapel steps. "He said, 'Good. Tell him to pay attention to how it ends—not with whether you win or lose, but with understanding.'"

The fog was burning off and revealed a clear blue sky above the bay. Sam was thinking that somewhere on the long road behind them, the young prosecutors were still standing in front of Phil's map, connecting dots that everyone else had learned to ignore. Still believing that the law could serve truth as well as power. Still planting gardens in hard soil.

Gus paused at the chapel door, running his hand over the faded red strings on Phil's map. "Ready?" he asked.

Sam thought about everything he had learned about truth and stories, and about the battles that matter even when they're lost. About how some quests don't end just because the knight does.

"Yeah," Sam said. "I'm ready."

They walked into the chapel together, while outside, the last of the fog lifted from San Francisco Bay, revealing the city in all its clear, complex truth.

After the service, after the sun had dropped behind the mountains, they walked back to their parked bikes. Sam had been quiet all evening, turning over the questions in his mind, the gaps in the story.

"You never told me how it ended," Sam finally said. "The real ending. Not the hero version."

Gus was quiet for a long moment.

"We got the indictment," he said finally. "Grand jury saw the evidence, heard the testimony. Phil presented for two weeks straight. Death certificates, internal memos, statistical analyses. The works." He paused for a second. "They returned a true bill. In the indictment there were multiple counts of criminally negligent homicide against Peterson Energy and three of its top executives."

"But?"

"But two weeks later, New Mexico elected a new attorney general. James Richardson III." Gus's voice took on an edge Sam hadn't heard before. "His campaign was largely funded by energy industry donations. Peterson Energy's PAC alone contributed a hundred thousand dollars."

"You're kidding!" Sam exclaimed.

"First day in office," Gus continued, "he called Phil in for a meeting. Said he'd reviewed the case and found it 'legally insufficient.' Ordered it dismissed." He laughed, but there was no humor in it. "Used words like 'prosecutorial overreach' and 'hostile business environment.' Said New Mexico needed to be more 'energy industry friendly.'"

"Could he do that? Just dismiss an indictment?"

"Attorney General has that power. Phil argued, of course. Brought in the evidence, the experts, the families of victims. Richardson didn't even pretend to listen." Gus turned toward his bike and reached into the tank bag for his water bottle, but found the bottle empty. "Week after the dismissal, Peterson Energy announced a major expansion of their operations. Richardson attended the groundbreaking ceremony."

Sam thought about Don Quixote, about how his greatest enemies weren't the giants themselves, but the enchanters who made everyone else see them as windmills.

"So that's why there's no record," Sam said. "The case just... disappeared."

"Not disappeared. Buried. There's a difference." He pulled something from his saddlebag—a thick manila envelope, worn at the edges. "Phil kept copies of everything. The evidence, the witness transcripts, the indictment. The truth doesn't go away just because someone puts it in a drawer."

"But it didn't matter in the end. The coal company won."

"Did they?" He handed Sam the envelope. "Look inside."

Sam placed it on the seat of his bike and opened it. In the dim light, he could see graphs, charts, testimony transcripts. But what caught his eye were more recent documents—news articles about climate change lawsuits, criminal investigations into corporate pollution, congressional hearings on industry deception.

"Everything Phil tried to prove," Gus said, "everything they called him crazy for saying—it's all accepted fact now. The companies knew. They lied. They chose profit over people. The only difference is that Phil saw it thirty years before everyone else caught up."

"But the case was dismissed."

Gus was quiet for a moment, letting the words settle. "Phil used to say that some battles need to be fought even if you know you'll lose, because fighting them changes what people think is possible."

"Yeah, but he lost."

"He lost the battle. But the war?" Gus gestured at the papers. "The truth has a way of surviving. Of finding new knights to fight for it."

Sam picked up one of the older documents—a Peterson Energy internal memo from 1973 calculating expected mortality rates in exposed communities. The paper was yellowed, but the words were clear as day. The truth preserved, waiting to be found.

"Why didn't you tell me this part earlier?" Sam asked. "About Richardson and the dismissal?"

"Because I needed you to understand what we were fighting first. What Phil saw, what he tried to do." Gus paused before adding, "Sometimes you have to believe in the quest before you can face how it ends."

Sam was silent for a full minute. Then he looked at his

grandfather, "You know what's interesting about Don Quixote? Everyone remembers that he loses. That the giants are really windmills. But they forget why he keeps fighting anyway."

"Why does he?"

"Because someone has to say what they really are. Even if no one believes it. Even if they can't win." Sam looked at the papers scattered around him, three decades of truth that never made the headlines. "Even if the story gets buried in the end."

Gus smiled, and for a moment Sam saw him as he must have been forty years ago, young and angry and ready to take on the giants.

"The story's not over, Sam. Richardson dismissed the case, but he couldn't bury the truth. Look around." He gestured at the horizon. "The giants are still here. They're just waiting for the next knight crazy enough to name them for what they are."

Sam carefully gathered the papers and put them back in their envelope. They were pieces of a story that hadn't ended, just gone underground like seeds waiting for the right season to grow.

CHAPTER 23

TRUTH

After Phil's service, Gus and Sam went to a motel on the outskirts of San Francisco. The fog had followed them inland, turning the parking lot lights into floating orbs. Sam couldn't sleep, his mind too full of the day's revelations, of the stories he'd heard at the service—some matching Gus's tales, others different in small but nagging ways.

In his earbuds, Don Quixote was in his final days, trying to explain to Sancho that everything he'd seen had been real, despite what enchanters made others believe. Sam looked over from his chair and repeated it to Gus.

Friend Sancho, by the same Creator who gave life to my soul, I tell you what I see is as real as you are real. These are no enchantments, but things of our world that have been twisted to appear otherwise to those who refuse to see their true nature.

Gus smiled. "That sounds like something Phil would

say about those corporate documents—about how the truth was there all along, just hidden by those who didn't want others to see it."

"It's like what we've seen on this trip," Sam said. "All these environmental disasters, all this damage—it's right there in front of everyone. But people choose to see what they want to see. Like calling climate change a natural cycle, or calling pollution the price of progress."

"Don Quixote saw giants where others saw windmills," Gus nodded his head in agreement. "Phil saw corporate murder where others saw business as usual. Sometimes seeing the truth means being willing to look crazy to everyone else."

Sam thought about Phil's map with its red strings, about Gus's stories of legal battles and buried evidence. About how memory and truth get tangled over time, like string unwinding from its spool.

Gus got up and went for a walk, clearly restless after the funeral service. His saddlebag laid open on his bed with papers spilling out—thirty years of carrying around pieces of a story Sam still wasn't sure he totally believed. Sam went to tuck them back in, and that's when he saw it: a yellowed newspaper clipping that had slipped behind the bedside table.

The paper was the *Albuquerque Journal*, dated March 15, 1985. The headline made his heart stop:

GRAND JURY INDICTS ENERGY GIANTS ON HOMICIDE CHARGES: Prosecutor Claims Companies *"Knowingly Caused Deaths" Through Pollution*

Sam's hands were shaking as he read:

"In an unprecedented legal action, the New Mexico Attorney General's office has secured grand jury indictments against Peterson Energy Corporation and three of its top executives on charges of criminally negligent homicide. Lead prosecutor Phil Stone alleges the company knowingly concealed evidence of fatal health impacts from air pollution and climate change...

...The indictments follow a two-week grand jury presentation of internal corporate documents and expert testimony...

...Peterson Energy spokesman calls charges 'bizarre and politically motivated'...

...Legal experts question viability of novel prosecution theory..."

And then, tucked at the bottom of the page, a smaller article dated two weeks later:

NEW AG DISMISSES PETERSON ENERGY CASE: Richardson Cites *"Insufficient Evidence"* For Controversial Charges

"The newly elected Attorney General, James Richardson III, today ordered the dismissal of all criminal charges against Peterson Energy Corporation, calling the case 'legally

insufficient' and harmful to New Mexico's business climate. The dismissal comes two days after Richardson's inauguration and effectively ends the controversial prosecution...

...Richardson's campaign received significant support from energy industry political action committees..."

The door opened. Gus stood there, silhouetted against the fog-diffused parking lot lights.

"Found it, did you?" he asked quietly.

"It was real." Sam's voice sounded strange to his own ears. "All of it. The case, the indictments, Phil..."

"Did you think I was making it up?" There was no accusation in his voice, just curiosity.

"I didn't know." Sam looked down at the clipping in his hands. "Everything's felt like Don Quixote lately—giants and windmills, truth that might be delusion. Even at the funeral today, the stories everyone told... some matched yours, some didn't."

"Memory's like that." He sat down heavily on his bed. "Everyone sees their own version of the truth. Even newspapers only tell part of the story."

"But this happened." Sam held up the article. "They really indicted them. You guys really did it."

"He really did." Gus smiled sadly. "For two weeks, David actually fought Goliath. For two weeks, someone called the giants what they really were."

"And then?"

"And then the giants reminded everyone that they

were just windmills. That Phil was crazy. That people like Richardson understood how the world really worked." He took the clipping from Sam's hands, looked at it like he was seeing an old friend. "Within a month, you could barely find anyone who remembered it had happened at all."

In Sam's earbuds, paused hours ago, Don Quixote was still trying to explain his truth to a world that had chosen not to see it. Sam thought about how stories survive—in yellowed newspapers, in faded maps, in memories that don't quite match but all point to something real.

"Why did you keep it?" Sam asked. "The article?"

"Because sometimes you need proof. Not for others, but for yourself. Proof that you weren't crazy, that you really saw what you saw." He carefully folded the clipping. "And because someone needs to remember that for two weeks in 1987, the truth was stronger than power."

Outside, the fog pressed against the window like something that was alive, transforming the world into something dreamlike. But the paper in Gus's hands was solid, real—a piece of truth that had survived its own ending.

"You know what *Don Quixote* really is?" Sam said suddenly. "It's not about someone who sees things that aren't there. It's about someone who remembers what everyone else has chosen to forget."

Gus looked at Sam for a long moment, then handed him the article. "Keep it," he said. "Someone needs to remember. Someone needs to know that truth can look like madness, and that sometimes the craziest thing is pretending not to see what's right in front of us."

Sam tucked the clipping into his copy of *Don Quixote*, between the pages where the knight first sees his giants on the horizon. Proof that sometimes, just sometimes, the giants are real and that someone needs to fight them.

The next morning, Sam stepped out of the motel room and joined his grandfather, who was standing next to the fully loaded motorcycles in the parking lot. "Ready to roll?" he asked his young partner.

Sam took a minute to check the cables, the oil level and tire pressure on his metal steed before starting its engine and throwing his right leg over the saddle. As he double checked his mirrors and pulled in the clutch, Sam glanced over at Gus who indicated he was ready to go. Sam pulled up next to his grandfather before they took off.

"What's up?" Gus asked.

Sam leaned forward, "I see it now," he said.

"What do you see?"

"I see something to fight for." Sam then placed his hand on top of the bike's headlight, as on the head of a faithful work horse, patted it lightly and added with a grin, "And I wanted you to know that I've named her Rocinante."

With a smile Gus nodded his head. With a twist of the throttle, they turned to the right and accelerated down the road.

About the Author

Michael Hemenway works as a defense attorney in Charlottesville, Virginia, and over the years has represented hundreds of clients from all walks of life. He has previously written two novels as well as a criminal justice primer.